About the Author

Joshua Hickford is an academic of modern history, who has a keen interest in the Second World War. He has always been interested in encapsulating the insanity of conflict, and how it weighs on the mind of its participants. *Retracting Claws* demonstrates his first foray into historical fiction, in an attempt to reflect the loss of reason and hopelessness felt by soldiers in the final days of WWII, and how they tried to come to terms with it.

Retracting Claws

Joshua Hickford

Retracting Claws

Olympia Publishers
London

www.olympiapublishers.com
OLYMPIA PAPERBACK EDITION

Copyright © Joshua Hickford 2023

The right of Joshua Hickford to be identified as author of
this work has been asserted in accordance with sections 77 and 78
of the Copyright, Designs and Patents Act 1988.

All Rights Reserved

No reproduction, copy or transmission of this publication
may be made without written permission.
No paragraph of this publication may be reproduced,
copied or transmitted save with the written permission of the
publisher, or in accordance with the provisions
of the Copyright Act 1956 (as amended).

Any person who commits any unauthorised act in relation to
this publication may be liable to criminal
prosecution and civil claims for damage.

A CIP catalogue record for this title is
available from the British Library.

ISBN: 978-1-80074-881-1

This is a work of fiction.
Names, characters, places and incidents originate from the writer's
imagination. Any resemblance to actual persons, living or dead, is
purely coincidental.

First Published in 2023

Olympia Publishers
Tallis House
2 Tallis Street
London
EC4Y 0AB

Printed in Great Britain

Chapter 1
109.5 Kilometres From Berlin

"Here should do fine," came the barked order, instructing Otto to bring the tank to a halt. Hauptmann Fritz Greim surveyed the scene of destruction before him, before marshalling the crew to salvage whatever they could from the destroyed SS Panzer column. Otto clutched his MP40, and proceeded to fling open the driver's hatch above his head. The cold of the April air was positively bracing when compared with the humid stuffiness of the crew cabin. Of greater shock, however, was the smell. Burning fuel, gunpowder, and scorched metal, mixed with clotting blood and singed flesh. How could this hell on the ground be mixed with such tranquillity above? A lone falcon flittered above the treetops, dominating the small prey that darted between the trees, in much the same fashion that Otto and his crew's own PzKpw VI Tiger I once proudly patrolled the Eastern Steppe with the arrogance only ever displayed by an alpha predator. Yet a once such proud beast as this machine was reduced to scavenging ammunition and fuel from mangled lumps of steel which once represented the pride of the Wehrmacht and SS, as it limped its way westwards to join the Berlin defence.

But now was not the time for such sentiments. The Soviets would be certain to send further reconnaissance patrols through the area, and so time for gathering sufficient supplies was short. He drew a sharp breath and hauled himself from the tank, hearing the clack of his machine pistol upon the armoured plating and the squelch of his boots as he dropped to the churned muddy ground.

"Gefreiter Otto Griff; check that nearest one," snapped Greim, with all his usual military formality.

Greim had only been their commander since his own Panther was knocked out in February, replacing their former commander, Von Stoltz, who had been injured by a particularly nasty piece of T-34 shell shrapnel. Stoltz was always a far more relaxed commander, not least due to the crew's relative luck since first deployed in Africa back in 1942. Greim had never had the same warmth that Stoltz had portrayed, yet Otto did feel an element of safety in the new commander's regimented stance. Hans Raeder was the crew's other new addition, after their previous radio operator Hermann Baum had rather swiftly bled to death from the same shell to which Stoltz had fallen victim. Raeder, however, was a somewhat less than level-headed and ordered individual; a boy of barely eighteen, he had been reduced from avid national socialist to nervous wreck following his first engagement alongside the crew.

Mounting the nearest destroyed tank with a grunt, Otto heaved open the hatch above the turret. Lowering himself in, he attempted to gain a foothold on the driver's seat, but his mud-laden boots offered a pitiful grip, and he slipped. A series of brassy clanks rank out across the tank, as it became apparent to Otto that he had, in his descent, caught the ammo rack and caused a spillage of shells. It seemed he was luckily unharmed despite such a harsh fall, and so he attempted to regain his bearings. The scene around him was deeply unsettling. Cold.

Lifeless. Unimaginably different to the stuffy and cramped cabin to which he had become accustomed. Most of the crew had managed to get out in time, with only the shredded corpse of the driver remaining. A shell had torn through this tank's rear during the previous battle, yet this was still wedged in the engine block – some rounds from an IL-2 tank hunter appear to have delivered the coup de grace, splitting the driver's neck and torso. Otto always found it particularly chilling to see fellow Wehrmacht or even SS drivers in such an unfortunate state, particularly as it was a position in which he could well find himself someday soon.

Mustn't dwell. His tank had protected him all the way up to April 1945, there was no point suggesting that it wouldn't carry him until this blasted war ended. Otto loaded his hessian sack with as many shells as he could reasonably manage, and climbed back out of the crippled Tiger. He could see Kellerman and Raeder returning with two jerry cans of fuel each, scavenged from a tank with a presumably in-tact engine. Isaac Kellerman was an odd sort of fellow. Part of the original crew, Kellerman had often been relatively calm in much the same fashion as Stoltz. He had, however, been very close friends with Baum; after he died in such a horrible fashion, something died within Kellerman also. He was distant, quick to anger, and his personality seemed to match the grotesque facial scar he bore from the T-34's shell. He seemed furious that Baum was taken and Stoltz invalided while he himself was lucky enough as to only receive a minor laceration. His anger was ever greater towards Raeder, whom he regarded with increasing disdain as a poor replacement for his dear friend Baum.

Otto once again trudged towards his Tiger, his bag of

shells in tow. Yet a sound was penetrating the early morning mist, bothering him. There was the usual distant drumfire of artillery, the steadily burning fuel of destroyed tanks, even the occasional muffled explosion of the fire travelling to ammunition storages. But unlike these anthems of war, the sound greeting Otto's ears was one which he had not yet, try as he might, been able to block out; it was a moan for help. He turned to the direction of the cries, and soon saw their origin: an SS Panzer gunner, propped against the tracks of his destroyed Panther. The dead sent a light chill through Otto, but the soon-to-be dead were positively blood curdling. And this man was indeed not long for this world – the size of the wound in his abdomen would suggest that he had caught the lion's share of a shell when trying to escape his tank. A trail of blood led from the escape hatch to where he lay, with much having begun to saturate the ground around him into a red putty, providing a striking contrast to his ghostly white face. What could Otto hope to do for this man? Put him out of his misery? He clicked the magazine release on his MP40 to see how many shots he had left. Five miserable rounds. Five! He could not waste one on this poor man before him. Otto simply retrieved a canteen of water from the knocked-out tank against which the man rested, gave it to the man along with a mumbled apology, and was careful to avoid eye contact as he turned towards his own Tiger. The soldier's cries had degenerated into incoherent, animal-like whimpers, which became ever fainter as he made the short walk back to his own tank.

"Get much?" inquired Peter Scholl from the turret. The crew's original gunner, Scholl provided a sense of constancy and calm, with his seemingly ever smiling manner a welcome break from the hell through which they often had to venture.

"Not as much as you, I'm sure," grinned Otto. Peter held five arrogant fingers aloft with a smirk. Otto glanced into his shell bag. Four, damn. Otto went to grudgingly inform Scholl of his failure, yet was distracted by a growing cloud of dust across the brow of the hill bordering the field on which the tank graveyard lay, a cloud soon peppered with small, blocky silhouettes. A Soviet reconnaissance patrol!

Greim was already calling the crew to action: "Griff, get back to the Tiger!"

Otto broke into a sprint, his shell bag over his shoulder and digging into his back. He dived aboard the tank, jumped into his seat with his shells and closed the hatch behind him.

There was scarcely room in the cabin for Otto, who was not an especially large man, to fit alongside his shells he had retrieved. He was aware he should pass them to Kellerman, who had arrived back to the tank along with Raeder while Otto was tending the SS tanker, but dared not move, so paralysed was he by the sight of the approaching enemy armour.

"Drive for God's sake, drive!" cried Raeder, seated adjacent to Otto, only to be greeted by a harsh blow to the back of the head by Kellerman.

"Quiet, you fool! What's your plan, just set off in front of an entire Soviet scouting party? With a pitiful three shells to our name? Have some sense man! We sit still and quiet and wait for them to pass."

Greim nodded concurrence, and so the crew braced themselves in hope of remaining undetected. They were well blended in to the destroyed panzer column, and so with fortune on their side the Reds should simply pass them by.

The rumble of the armour grew continuously stronger, with the spent bullet casings which littered the floor of the tiger beginning to tremor until they grew into a tin-like orchestra. Otto's grip on the steering wheel of the panzer was like iron, with his hands coated in sweat, as he prepared to move the Tiger with the greatest possible speed at a moment's notice, should they be discovered. Kellerman gripped the next shell to be fired, Scholl remained glued to the gunsight, all ready to leap into action; Raeder nervously quivered, as had become the norm. Finally, Otto caught sight of one the party out of the corner of his driver's sight. Two T-34s, loaded with Soviet personnel. The first drove past with little issue, continuing down the sloped field towards the treeline.

The second tank stopped. Otto felt his hands turn to ice, and could hear his heart pounding in his ears. Had they been spotted? The Soviets weren't looking at their tank however, nor were they in a state of combat readiness; they were looking at the still-dying man by whom Otto had stopped to give water. They were jeering and joking with one another as they approached him. They then began a vile display of kicking the dying man, jabbing his wounds until his whimpers grew into almighty shrieks and howls. This all only ceased when a stern-sounding Russian officer opened the tank hatch and yelled at them, precipitating a hurry back to the tank as he pulled out his pistol and shot the man. But he did not move or flinch, only jolted as the bullet found him; the man had fainted from the pain already. It was always hard for Otto to know what to make of the SS men he saw. He was torn with conflict; he had heard rumours of terrible crimes committed by the SS, though only whispers had reached him, which would follow that they deserved such reprisals. But who was to say that this individual man was culpable? How could one tell the guilty from the innocent? There was no way he could know. However, so many questions of what was sane anymore had arisen in these years of retreat that Otto could not dwell on such conundrums for long, lest he go insane much like Raeder.

By the time Otto returned to the present the second tank was leaving, and the crew were giving a sigh of relief. He began to feed power into the Tiger's engine, feeling the tremendous roar of the engine coughing to life.

"Move us into the treeline, Gefreiter Griff. We need to keep moving West and join the Berlin defence, if only we can slip past these damned Soviets that are closing on the city. Kellerman, how many shells?"

"Twelve, Herr Hauptman," replied Kellerman.

Greim merely rubbed his brow and grunted approval. Otto threw revs at the Tiger, slipping it into gear and feeling the tank begin to jolt forward; the left track stiffer than the right, as usual. Such asymmetrical tracks were hardly unlikely, as the tank had thrown its left track twice in the past month owing to landmines. The initial roar of the engine now died to a lower pitch growl, as it was assisted by the Tiger's growing momentum.

The tank ran through the forest, until the trees began to grow less dense and Otto could make out some activity on the clearing just ahead. It was the two T-34s which had passed them in the graveyard, now stopped with the accompanying infantry eating in the midday sun. He proceeded cautiously to get a better view, and then ground the tank to a halt, turning to Greim for further instructions.

"We will have to go forward," asserted Greim. "We will only keep running into them, or they'll report our position to artillery."

"Surely we can just go around, Herr Hauptman?" pleaded

Raeder. Yet again he was answered by Kellerman's fist to the back of his head. Otto felt sorry for the poor boy but couldn't help let out a chuckle at Kellerman's response. Ignoring the comment of Raeder, Greim continued.

"Scholl, fire at the tank on the left first. We have a clear view of their side, and should knock out the crew in one hit. Griff, as soon as the shot is fired, move us forward. Wait on my command to release the throttle and pull only the right brake – this should turn us to a forty-five-degree angle from the second, with their shell deflecting off our armour and giving us time to fire."

Otto could not help but be impressed by Greim's tremendous efficiency. A swift battle plan, worked in seconds. While he missed Stoltz greatly, he could not but entertain the growing feeling that Greim was the one to lead them back to Berlin in one piece. Kellerman readied a second shell, Scholl took aim, and Otto prepared to move, while Raeder continued to cower. It was perhaps unfair to expect much from Raeder at this stage; the Tiger's radio had been knocked out a few days previously, and until they salvaged a working one, he was largely redundant, a spare part. Having no job to attend aboard the Tiger seemed to affect one's nerves rather negatively, as they could no longer convince themselves that they were in any control of their own fate, but had to simply rely upon the others around them.

The turret stopped moving, indicating that Scholl had lined up the Tiger's prey. He paused a moment, and then unleashed its bite. The sound shuddered through the cabin; most noises were soon replaced by a ringing of the ears which one never quite got used to. It bounced through the trees, feeding the sound back to the crew several times over. The

Russian tank began producing smoke, and yielded no movement, which implied that Scholl had probably hit the majority of its occupants. Greim had, rather fearlessly, opened his hatch to man the MG 42 atop the turret, firing into the gathered Soviet troops as they tried to orientate themselves. Otto was already moving the tank, as if by instinct, waiting for a signal from Greim. Even Raeder had seemed to briefly compose himself enough to fire blindly into gatherings of enemy troops. Small arms fire began to now ping against the Tiger's armour, yet this was of little concern to the crew; the concern was the second T-34, whose turret was rotating towards them.

Just moments before the main gun of the Soviet tank found them, Greim kicked Otto's shoulder, the signal which had become normal in the crew to avoid voice commands being lost in the music of battle. As instructed, Otto reduced the throttle and pulled hard on the right-hand brake. As Greim had planned, the tank jerked to a halt on its right, with the left track carrying it just far enough to provide an incline to the enemy fire. Nor was it a moment too soon either; a white puff billowed from the barrel of the T-34, followed by the crack of a shot. The shell impacted the Tiger's front with an almighty and ringing prang, as the projectile deflected and struck the earth some way to the Tiger's right. All the while, Kellerman had been labouring to replace the spent round in the turret, and tapped Scholz that it was ready moments after the T-34 had spent its own shell. The Tiger fired once more, with the round entering the enemy vehicle just to the right of the turret centre. This did not produce a mere stack of black smoke like the first tank, but an almighty orange explosion as its top half was thrown some distance into the air, from what one could assume to be an exploded ammo rack, paired with the expected thunderous boom.

The crew now turned their attention to the foot soldiers. Many had been killed before they knew from where they were being attacked. Out of a roughly twenty which had been part of the reconnaissance party, only a handful of around five men had gathered themselves enough to put up effective resistance. The machine guns of Greim and Raeder continued to fire, until only a pair were left, who swiftly dropped their weapons and ran for the treeline at the other end of the clearing, using the knocked out first T-34 as cover. Greim showed no wish to pursue them; Otto could only assume this was because by the time that they reported our position to the next Soviet formation, we would be gone. After a brief survey of the field in front of us, Greim gave the order to scavenge what could be taken, and for the second time in only a few hours Otto left his drivers compartment and began to move towards the enemy encampment.

Otto approached the area with great apprehension; how could he be sure that all who lay still were dead? This damned war had shown him great feats of human endurance, and summoning the energy to put up a fight after having been shot was well within the means of a Red Army soldier. And while the second T-34 could be safely written off with regard to surviving occupants, the smoking yet unexploded first tank was far from such certainty. Kellerman was ahead of Otto, his eyes locked on the as yet unopened T-34 hatch with his weapon aimed. Otto climbed aboard one side of the enemy tank and met Kellerman on top of the turret, careful to maintain silence and hear any movements inside. And movements there were. A faint but definite laboured breathing just below the driver's hatch, a groaning from the turret, and Russian whispers interspersed with winces.

Otto stared at Kellerman in alarm. But his gaze was met by Isaac Kellerman's usual huntsman-like focus, as he mouthed to Otto that he needed a grenade. Otto was always terrified of Kellerman's stare, though he would never tell him so. Very little blinking. Shark-like. Some sort of wild glare only present in those whose first casualty of this war had been their reason. Someone who had been long dying inside while the body carried on, a well-oiled killing machine, not unlike the Tiger they crewed.

Otto came back to his senses and fumbled his equipment belt for a stick grenade. Unhooking it, he unscrewed the cap and passed it to Kellerman. In one swift movement, he pulled the priming pin and, opening the hatch just enough for the charge to fit through, dropped it into the enemy tank. He slammed the lid shut once more, and both he and Otto held it closed with all their might. A moment after the grenade clanked to the tank floor, the Russian whispers grew into panicked shouts, with the turret escape hatch being pushed against and almost overcoming the full weight of both Otto and Kellerman. A muffled blast and small tremor, and the tank fell silent.

Kellerman departed without saying a word, beginning to search the bodies and ammunition crates of the fallen Russians. This left the task of checking the grotesque mess which had been created inside the green shell of the T-34 to Otto. He waited a moment to be sure that there was no more noise inside, before opening the hatch, MP40 at the ready. He didn't need it. The stench of blood washed over Otto, intermingling with the choking smoke from the Tiger's mauling. A brief look at the crimson explosion inside the turret told Otto all he could ever need to know. He dropped the hatch back into place and drew a sharp breath. Despite all he had seen, he found a certain level of comfort being behind his driver's periscope. There was always something separating him from the horror he was inflicting. But such a hands-on, open confrontation with death like this was still enough to drain the strength from his legs, and make his vision blur slightly.

He had little recovery time. A thunderous bang echoed through the trees, and reverberated through the tank on which Otto sat. Or rather was sitting – before he had properly registered the sound, he had instinctively flung himself to the grassy clearing below. Landing with a dull thud, and a pain shooting through his side which he barely even had time to register, Otto scanned the treeline to the direction from which he thought that the sound had come. Eventually he caught sight of another plume of white smoke, as yet another Russian T-34 rolled into view from the treeline. The shot, Otto believed, had whistled just past him; an explosion of soil and grass a number of metres behind him confirmed the hypothesis.

Otto remained on the ground, and soon loosed his five measly rounds in the general direction of his aggressor. A hollow clack demonstrated to him that his weapon had run dry, and so he cast it aside and ran to cower behind the hulk of the crippled tank which he was attending. His own Tiger now fired at the enemy tank, which had clearly not seen it in the treeline at first instance. The shot ricocheted off of the frontal armour, an unusual miss for Scholl, who had likely been shocked by its sudden appearance. The Russian machine now turned to face the Tiger, however, and its entry from the treeline had facilitated an almost perfect angle of fire, perpendicular to the side armour. Without Otto to drive to a better position, or Kellerman to assist faster loading, the likelihood was that the shell would penetrate the armour and kill some of his fellow crewmen. Powerless to help, Otto simply had to sit and watch as the Russian stopped moving and finished aiming at his own tank, while the machine gunner kept Otto and Kellerman firmly glued to their cover. There followed another great boom, and Otto looked for the tell-tale white smoke pillar indicating a shot fired from the T-34.

But there was none. The machine guns had fell silent, and a small number of flames began to lick upwards from just behind the enemy tank. Why hadn't it fired? Had he not heard the sound of a shot? Otto took a moment to think, and he realised that the second shot, the one aimed at the Tiger, was quite different in sound to the first which narrowly missed him; it was higher, with a less bass-heavy boom than could be expected. Glancing at Kellerman, who had taken cover behind some crates nearby, Otto registered the same sense of bewilderment upon his face as he too wondered what the sound was. This brief moment of quiet, following the mysterious noise, was soon punctured by gunfire and shouts, but not in Russian – in German. The gunfire, too, was not the sound of Russian Mosin-Nagant rifles and PPSH41 machine guns, but German assault rifles.

Otto raised his head above the frontal armour of the destroyed tank to see the scene more completely – and what a scene it was. A group of SS camouflage-clad soldiers were darting out of the treeline behind the T-34, firing towards the hatches to prevent the Soviets from rising to return fire. They began to climb the still active tank, which they seemed to have crippled with a Panzerfaust, accounting for the sound which Otto had heard. One of them wrenched open the hatch, only to be shot twice from the inside. The man fell from the tank, clutching his neck, and writhed on the floor for a short time before growing still. A second man jumped to his place, and fired his rifle several times into the open hatch. Another troop had got to the driver's entrance, which he flung open and dragged out a surrendering young man. He seemed around the age of Raeder, by his appearance, and in a similar state to Raeder's almost perpetual hysteria.

When the gunfire ceased, Otto and Kellerman began to step towards the SS group. The Russian driver was still begging for his life, according to his tone, on the floor next to the shot SS teenager who was by now quite dead. Damn kids. They simply run at targets without any shadow of the cautious approach to clearing tanks which himself and Kellerman had displayed not five minutes previously. Such wasted life, a trend which had only seemed to grow increasingly common the further they retreated into German territory. Combine desperation with the ham-fisted brutality of the Waffen SS, and these could be the only results.

"We had been tracking that damned T-34 for days and had set up the perfect ambush before you lumbered into the vicinity," reprimanded the SS leader. "The crew must've heard the shots from your little scuffle, as they quickly changed direction and made their way towards here."

"Killing too many tanks for you, were we?" jeered Scholl from the now opened turret hatch of the Tiger. Otto allowed himself a chuckle; it was always satisfying to see the arrogant SS put in their place. Even Raeder was laughing.

Otto's gaze now turned to the Russian driver on the

ground. What could they do with him? They would never make it back to the German lines with a prisoner in transit, yet they couldn't shoot a surrendering prisoner.

"Are you going to let the poor boy go? There's no sense shooting prisoners, and two Reds already slipped us earlier."

The SS man nodded approval and gestured to the boy to run. When he had only covered about ten metres, the officer drew his pistol and shot the runner in the back, just below the right shoulder blade. Otto could barely comprehend such barbarism, as the young man crumpled to the floor and moved about slowly. He shot a furious look at the SS officer, and ran to the Russian. The shot had entered the back and torn out the majority of the lung, and the boy, who had now rolled to face Otto, was choking on blood. Otto cradled the young man's head, which was contorted with a mix of pain and fear. He put pressure on the exit wound, but was well aware that nothing could be done for him at this stage; the SS officer's aim was deadly in the extreme.

Within seconds, the choking slowed, and the boys clasp on Otto's tunic released. Otto turned away from the diluting eyes; staring death in the face could only alter one's mind for the worse. Meanwhile, Greim had dismounted the Panzer and was yelling furiously at the SS man, who was stood to attention at Greim's superior rank. His grudging acceptance of Greim's authority was likely eased by his imposing figure; a man of well over six foot, Greim was able to combine his formal military bearing with a close and overbearing physique to scare obedience out of any subordinate rank, no matter their arrogance. He could barely fit inside the tank. Otto removed himself from the increasingly cold corpse which lay before him, and trudged back to his drivers position in the Tiger. He passed the still yelling Greim, without listening to what was said. Suffice to say it was the ticking off of a lifetime.

Even Scholl's usual beaming smile had been replaced with grave seriousness having seen the slaughter of the Russian driver. He made no boyish quip, no joke setup, but simply gave a look of sympathy in Otto's direction. Otto could barely meet his eyes; what was he fighting for anymore? A crumbling regime which happily killed defenceless innocents? How could this still be the Germany he was so proud to be defending when he had first donned his panzer cap in the Summer of 1942, ready to take Stalingrad? Opening his hatch, he found that Raeder had been busy checking the Soviet positions during the drama, and had found a captured MP40 magazine to leave on his seat. Picking it up, the weight indicated to Otto that it was full. A luxury. He felt free, finally able to fire without every shot being his last.

"Thanks, Raeder," said Otto, through the whisper of a smile which he finally felt he could regain. Perhaps Raeder had been reduced to the shadow of a Tiger crewman, but he was indeed a good lad. A young man of eighteen, he could still provide evidence that human decency remained in this world. Raeder shot a nervous smile, but a warm one nevertheless.

Kellerman tapped Hans and said, "Here, take this. You need to eat something, I haven't seen you eat all day," handing him a roll he had evidently pillaged from the Soviet crates.

While he was certainly not a fan of Raeder, Kellerman could not shirk his fatherly instinct. The oldest of the crew in his mid-30s, Isaac had once been father to a teenage boy at home, who had perished to a Lancaster bomb in 1943. Otto failed to shake the feeling that Raeder reminded Kellerman of his own son in some ways, possibly explaining his harsh behaviour.

The turret hatch opened, and Greim dropped back into the tank. "They were trying to disrupt the Russian supply lines before they got near Berlin. Terrible man, classical SS arrogance," he informed the crew, with no lack of contempt in his voice. "We should just keep moving West. We should make Berlin in a couple of days, allowing for the expected disruption of Soviet movements. Onwards, driver." Giving Otto a nod, he returned to his hatch to continue checking the view ahead of him. Otto once more fired up the mighty Tiger, and began moving to the other end of the clearing, careful to avoid the debris and tanks left in their wake. The metallic clunking and squeaking of the tracks sped up as Otto revved the engine, bringing the Tiger into a run.

Some time passed with little to say. The forest was, while beautiful, relatively uniform and monotonous. The occasional burnt-out shell of a Russian or German tank here, abandoned posts littered with green and grey uniformed corpses there. Suddenly, they burst out from the treeline into open country. The tank was moving at almost top speed, thundering across the war-stricken countryside with tremendous power. There seemed little cover or shelter available in the area, save the occasional farmhouse or barn.

Berlin was visible now, as they began to descend the hills of fields. His beloved home city was in a pitiful state. A blackened cloud hung perpetually above the historic settlement, and an iron ring of Soviet lines steadily closed its strangle hold on the suburbs. Otto wasn't quite sure how they were expecting to break into the city, though he knew Greim would have a plan for that. He couldn't help but remember when the rattle of the Panzer's tracks was replaced with the steady hum of the bus engine as he and his family went into town. He had lived in the inner section of the Seelow heights before the war, and he and his family had often journeyed East for family vacations and the like. The last he had heard, his family were evacuating Westwards into central Berlin, though he could hardly be certain. The crew had grown accustomed to incredibly sparse contact with home; with a country collapsing around them, the expectation of a working postal service was frankly fanciful.

Chapter 2
97.3 Kilometres From Berlin

The peaceful Journey was soon cut short by the gigantic prang of an anti-tank landmine, throwing the left track and causing the Tiger to grind to a halt. This did not alarm the crew, but rather infuriated them at the prospect of yet another afternoon tending the caterpillar belt. Even Raeder merely sighed; so familiar was the sound of a mine to the men that none feared that the sound would be anything resembling an enemy attack.

"For God's sake!" exclaimed Kellerman, striking the wall of the turret with his fist. As the mechanic, the responsibility would fall to him to repair the wounded Tiger. Greim massaged his brow, clearly trying to formulate a plan for how to best use the resources at his disposal. Within an instant, he sparked to life; raising his head, he rattled off a series of commands.

"Kellerman, begin work on the track with Scholl. Griff, Raeder, go check that nearest cottage for supplies," gesturing to a small farmer's house nearby.

Otto obediently swung open his hatch and climbed out of the tank. The warm afternoon sun was still strong, though a dark grey storm was looming in the distance, hanging ominously above the crew's hopes for a bit of dry weather to fix the track under. The country looked lifeless; the war so tangibly close in the smoke stacks of Berlin, yet just out of reach. The artillery beats constant, yet just far enough to provide a sense of quiet, of solitude. The chirping of birds in the trees had become muted, replaced by the howling wind of open countryside. Otto could only hear the breeze, and his own squelching footsteps as he wandered towards the hut. He did not approach with his usual method of caution; this area had been totally abandoned in the retreat to Berlin.

Surely enough, Raeder kicked open the door of the hut to reveal a scene of desolation. The shelves had been hurriedly cleared, as the occupants panicked to store their food, dropping the odd jar to shatter to the ground. Half packed bags rested on the bed with clothes strewn around them, where the owners had had to leave earlier than they thought. Open cupboards, emptied drawers, looted chests – all signs of the utter desperation that this war had wrought. Otto simply sighed and began searching for any food left behind. Tinned food was best, as it was less likely to be tainted by the oiled interior of the Tiger, and he could hardly stand yet another piece of bread which had been soaked in engine grease.

Kellerman could be heard cursing as he rummaged through his toolbox near the Tiger a few dozen yards away, as Scholl laughed at his anger incessantly, only exacerbating Kellerman's rage.

Raeder turned and asked, "Griff, there isn't much here. Do you mind checking the shed on the other side of the garden?"

Otto smiled and gave a nod, as Raeder seemed busy rifling through the cupboards. Lifting the latch on the back door of the cottage, Otto realised through the window of the door that there was some sort of black shadow in the branches of the garden tree, even darker than the approaching storm. Otto wandered if it might be a piece of debris or parachute, perhaps even a part of an aircraft? Opening the door fully, he was suddenly confronted by the face of what hung from the tree. A young man.

Otto recoiled at the sight. A man dressed in Wehrmacht uniform swung steadily from the tree from which he had been strung. He couldn't have been there more than a day, as the body showed no signs of decomposition setting in. Another unusual skill added to Otto's repertoire by this hellish war was the ability to gauge how long bodies had lain in the open, especially in these months of retreat. Around the neck of the body was a sign, reading, "I refused to fight for the German people" in German gothic font. SS monsters. Otto could only assume that the band of SS he had seen earlier were the culprits, likely triggered to violence by some perceived slight which in no way warranted this draconian response. Otto felt frozen in time for a moment, unable to take his eyes off the fallen soldier. Returning to his senses, his thoughts turned to Raeder; what would the poor lad think when he saw this? The strung-up man seemed to be perhaps even younger than Raeder, barely making sixteen. Raeder might be a man technically, but as the baby of the crew they all felt a responsibility to shield him from the worst horrors wherever they could, not least due to his nervous disposition.

Returning to the house, Otto sighted Raeder heaving his haversack over his shoulder with the clunk of tins.

"Managed a few tins and some medical supplies, and a little water," reported Raeder, clearly pleased with the haul he had gathered. Otto nodded distractedly, unable to shake the image of the hanged boy.

"Hans, why don't you go and set up some shelters and cooking stations near the tank? Looks like we will be staying the night," Otto said to Raeder.

Noticeably taken aback by Otto's use of Raeder's own first name, he simply obeyed without question. Following out of the cabin, Otto began to move towards the Tiger. The sun had begun to hide itself in the horizon, just peeking high enough to bounce its rays off the tank's scar-ridden armour. Scholl was still taunting Kellerman, who was by now wearing a rare smile himself and laughing along, while Greim studied a map.

Otto knew he had to bury the boy in the tree, but it would take far too long by himself. Kellerman would be able to dig the fastest whole, but showing the corpse of a boy around the age of Kellerman's late son might even wrench a tear from his stone heart. Instead, Otto caught the eyes of Scholl, and gestured to follow; Otto's grave expression prevented any question from Scholl of the necessity of his cooperation, and so he dismounted the tank without a word. The men did not talk on their short journey – Otto's demeanour had infected Scholl with sobriety, and he appeared aware that he was about to be confronted with something serious. Swinging open the back door once again, Otto still felt a stirring in his stomach at the dreadful crime in front of him. Scholl drew a sharp breath, and stepped back as if to steady himself.

"My God, what have those beasts done now?" exclaimed Scholl, with a more than palpable tone of dismay and confusion in his voice. After reading the attached placard, Scholl turned to Otto with a grim expression, commanding, "Go get the entrenching tools, will you? I'll cut him down, and we can try to give him a proper burial."

Otto made for the Tiger again, passing the still cursing Kellerman, who had once again turned his anger to Raeder for not setting the shelters up correctly. Reaching into a bag kept on the side of the tank, Otto drew two entrenching shovels, passing unnoticed by Hauptman Greim, who was still transfixed by his map.

By the time Otto arrived back in the garden, Scholl had laid the young man down, and removed both the rope and sign from his neck. Compared with the image which had previously greeted Otto in the tree, the boy looked strangely at peace now, lain carefully on his back with his hands settled on his chest, eyes closed. It was strange how a mere touch of human decency and respect could turn a horrific crime scene into a calm, though of course still tragic, resting place. Throwing Scholl one of the shovels, Otto began to dig into the grass adjacent the tree. It was soft, with the April rains having livened the soil, breathing life into the flora and fauna of the well-kept garden. Despite the fact that they were beginning to wilt at the lack of tending which they seem to have regularly received previously, the flowers across the garden provided a delightful display of colours and accompanying insect life. A sanctuary from the terror not a couple dozen miles away at the front, this garden was a peaceful reprieve for Otto and Scholl, and perhaps a brief last dignity for the poor hanged man, to be buried in such gorgeous surroundings.

The hours sped past, as Otto and Scholl laboured in the dirt. The night had begun to descend on the fields now, with the clear night sky revealing a dazzling array of stars. The image was punctuated by the AA searchlights in Berlin which danced across the night sky, blending seamlessly into the orange glow from the burning city, which irradiated the darkened skies above. Crickets and bugs of the garden were more than audible, being paired with yet not drowned out by the steady drone of the air raid warning sirens from Otto's own home city. It was always a mystery to Otto Griff as to how such a horrendous and increasingly pointless activity as this war could produce such beauty, such breath-taking scenes of bright and colourful days to be replaced by magical nights, at the expense of so much suffering. The sweating silhouettes of Otto and Scholl were painted upon the far wall, an orange hue encapsulating them as it leapt from the fire which Scholl had lit using the hateful placard, in order to provide some light for the two workers. After some time, enough to place the moon high above, they stopped.

"This seems deep enough to me. Let's get him in there," said Otto, with Scholl nodding agreement through quickened panting.

Together, they took either side of the boy's tunic and dragged him carefully into place, ensuring not to hit the head on the way down. Climbing back out of the grave, they began to push the heaped soil back into place, engulfing the young man until the ground became more or less level again. Otto removed his cap, holding it in front of him. Scholl turned to Otto and asked him to say a few words; a devout protestant for much of his childhood, he was versed in last rites.

"Lord, protect this poor boy… um…" said Otto, flicking open the identity papers to check his name. "This boy, Thomas Kerner, who was taken from us by the Devil's own. Please guard him against evil, and allow him a peaceful rest," cited Otto. After a moment's silence, he made one final adage. "And may Adolf Hitler rot in hell far before Thomas Kerner is sent there!" jested Otto. Scholl chuckled, and praised Otto for his words.

Just as the obituary finished, Otto turned to the door from

which he had come, only to see the overbearing figure of Greim in the doorway. He was sure to have heard Otto's little postscript insult, and have realised that they were undoing an SS crime, to the extent that it could be undone at least. Otto and Scholl braced for a verbal assault. Yet Greim did not have an expression of anger, but one of tacit approval. He merely nodded respectfully in their direction, and retreated into the house. Otto could only assume that even the warrior of Greim was battle weary, and beginning to see the futility of the task to which they were applying themselves. Fighting for a morally corrupt and dying regime, with even more corrupt and dying military formations. Otto glanced at Scholl, who merely shrugged and proceeded after Greim into the house, with Otto in tow. The Hauptman had set his map across one of the tables in the cottage, dimly lit by a candle, and was busy measuring and remeasuring routes and enemy positions, as he always seemed to be.

Otto, along with Peter Scholl, decided it best to leave Greim to his calculations, and went to join the rest of the crew. Raeder had managed to set a Zeltbahn against the tank, with a small campfire nearby, atop which mess tins were bubbling merrily away, with an unidentified food presumably inside. Kellerman was taking a well-earned rest by the fire, and was drawing languorously on his clay pipe for a job well done. He restricted his pipe smoking to special occasions, due to the collapse of the supply system to which the crew had been subjected for the past few weeks. Tobacco rations were rare in earnest; his care not to over use his precious supply, even after having successfully repaired a track to working order, could be told by his slow and savouring drags upon the smouldering tube. He and Raeder even seemed to be sharing an uncharacteristic joke, for they were both displaying broad smiles by the time Otto and Scholl joined them.

"Care for a turn?" asked Kellerman, directing his pipe at Otto. Otto held up a hand and shook his head in refusal; he hadn't quite shaken the lasting nausea of the grim undertaking he had just assisted in, combined with gnawing hunger. The same offer was made to Scholl, who laughed and reached for his own cigarettes.

"With you keeping your tobacco in your pants? I think I'll pass you damned animal!" giggled Scholl, sparking his match.

"Hey, got to do something to keep it dry!" retorted Kellerman through grinning teeth.

He finally made the offer to Raeder, of all people, who took the pipe with visible apprehension. A small suck upon it and he was reduced to a coughing, spluttering shape, trying to regain breath through his laughing. The rest of the crew were jeering him, as he handed the pipe back to a tickled Kellerman. After the laugh wore off, Kellerman produced a serious face.

"Raeder, you know you mustn't think too much about this war. It'll take your mind, it really will. Don't think about it," he said with his tone matching his darkened expression. Such an unexpected tonal shift and accompanying statement was not out of character for Kellerman; a deeply proud man, he would suddenly open up and reveal advice or observations only when he felt sufficiently relaxed, and a comradely atmosphere allowed it. He ended with a well-meaning pat on the back of Raeder, who nodded in agreement.

"You're right, I try not to dwell. But why are we even carrying on?"

What a question. The crew knew that anyone's answer for continuing in such madness would be insufficient to actually justify the insanity, but different from anyone else's motives. Kellerman breathed a puff of smoke and began to answer while staring into the fire almost longingly, as if it was a window to better times.

"Well, I don't know about you lot, but I need to justify myself to my son. Wilhelm was killed by a bomb at my own home, while I, who was at the dangerous front while he at the safe home, continue to survive. I feel the only way I can forgive myself for what happened is put up the best possible fight for the Russian until I'm told not to. If I tried to avoid duty and danger, regardless of the pointlessness of going through it, I'd never sleep again knowing that I dodged danger when my son fell in apparent safety. If I finish my service, then at least I know I've done all I can to repay my son's death," narrated Kellerman. He almost seemed to hold back a tear, yet masked it with a smile, and made a final comment, saying, "Sure it might not make sense to you lot. Hell, I'm not even sure it makes sense to me anymore. But there it is. Like I said, don't think about it."

Scholl was next up, as the crew's attention turned to him. He began. "Well, at first I bought into the propaganda, back in 1940. Defence of the German fatherland, repayment for 1918, you know. This changed to hopes of the 'Wunderwaffen', that maybe the vengeance weapons and King Tigers would turn things around." His face broke steadily into a smile as he continued to reminisce. "I even wanted to drive one! But it's become pretty clear that even they couldn't do it, and now I just hope that if we keep fighting, we will hold out long enough for a treaty rather than total destruction. The bottom line is hope. Because if I lose hope, I lose myself."

Otto didn't know how to respond to the two men. Both of

their justifications were simply so far removed from rationality. But they were justifications. What could one do to maintain sanity, or even the illusion of sanity, except hold onto anything tangible? This conflict had gone so far beyond reason that anyone would be forgiven for lacking a bit of logic in their ways of carrying on. The men then turned to him, gesturing him to give his own story. Why was Otto carrying on? He had always elected to simply ignore it, never dwell. He gathered his thoughts and tried to find the best way to articulate them to his fellow crewmates.

"I guess, it's all I've ever known," sighed Otto. "I barely remember civilian life. I served with this Tiger since 1942. At least while I was behind the wheel, I knew I could rely on steady enough rations, a crew having my back, and a powerful metal beast protecting me at every turn. Nowhere is truly safe anymore, let alone for a German. So, I just retreat into routine, and keep doing what I can rely on until I can't do it anymore." The crew were rendered speechless, as they could all at least partly relate to his monologue. They all had some sentiment attached to the repetitive nature of the task facing them from day to day.

A few moments of awkward silence hung over the campfire, only broken by the crackling of the wood. Finally, Scholl clapped his hands and exclaimed that the food was ready. Plain, boiled potatoes. Dull food had become the norm in the past few days, since the crew had been cut off from Berlin by a sudden Russian offensive, and had to last on only the provisions which they'd already packed or could scour from the landscape. Raeder, however, had brought his face into further grin, as he unwrapped a paper package he had produced from his pocket. He brought the paper aside to reveal a hefty enough chunk of salted meat.

"Where the hell did you get that?" cried Kellerman in joy, his eyes fixed on the mouth-watering morsel.

"It was in the house, when I was checking for supplies. Thought we could add it to our little feast," replied Raeder. He carefully sliced the meat with his combat knife into five pieces, distributing one to each of his fellow fire dwellers and keeping two himself, with one owed to Greim.

"Hans, this was a good find. Well done, lad," said Kellerman.

Raeder was practically glowing with the praise he had received from such a hard to please man as Kellerman. They savoured the meat like they'd never eaten anything but potato; this was, after all, how it had come to feel in the past few weeks anyway. It was tough, chewy, and barely seasoned, but for the exhausted Tiger crew it was all of their Christmases at once. After finishing, a still beaming Raeder went to deliver Greim's share.

By the time Raeder returned, he had Greim accompanying him. The officer approached the fire with his customary look of weighty responsibility. "You did well today men, and you've cause to celebrate. But I'm afraid I must cut the festivities short. The fire could be seen by a Russian patrol or aircraft, and you'll need some rest. We aren't going to stop for rest for the next two days, until we arrive in Berlin. Get some rest; I'll take first watch, then Raeder, Griff, Scholl and Kellerman, in that order. Alternate every hour and a half. Get some rest boys."

And with that, Fritz Greim drew his hunting rifle from the side of the tank and began scanning the horizon. The man had been a keen hunter before the war, and this was well reflected in the calm yet determined way in which he stalked potential prey. Otto threw the remaining water over the fire, and tucked up against the tracks, the sizzling of the logs still reverberating through the night air. He closed his eyes, trying to push the day's events out of mind, and drifted to sleep.

He didn't rest for long. He felt that it was only moments before he was being tapped awake by a whispering Raeder.

Rubbing his eyes, he asked, "Has it already been three hours?" in the drowsiest of mumbles.

"No, but there are two Soviets in that cottage we checked. In the darkness they must've thought our tank was just another knocked out wreck. I'm sorry to wake you, but…" whispered Raeder apologetically, trailing off assuming that Otto had taken his meaning. While annoyed his sleep had been cut short, Otto was glad that Raeder had woken him rather than try to deal with the Reds himself. He nodded tiredly, clasped his MP40, and followed Raeder to the cottage. Raeder had taken the Kar98 kept on the side of the tank, and they stalked towards the cottage. Russian chatting could be heard from inside, sounding relatively quiet. Candles had been lit inside, and shadows were darting across the window as the soldiers joked to each other inside.

After what felt like forever, they arrived at the door to the cottage. Raeder pushed on the handle, which unfortunately gave way with a definitive sound of tumblers moving. Raeder winced, and froze on the spot. The Russians had stopped talking. For a moment, they stood still, not daring to breathe, desperately waiting for another voice to arise inside the cottage. The next noise they heard was not a voice. The first man crashed through the door, breaking it and launching Raeder to the ground. He was pinning the young man, beating him with bestial grunts. Otto raised his machine pistol aloft, and pulled the trigger. Click. In his sleepy state, he had forgotten to cock the action of his MP40, and so the spring was not set, nor a round chambered. Idiot! Just as he was about to set the weapon, he observed another Russian in the doorway, as if in slow motion. He was readying his rifle, undoubtedly to take out either Otto or Raeder. In a heartbeat, Otto hurled his gun at the Russian and charged him. The weapon threw the man off balance, and Otto clattered into him, attempting to wrestle the rifle off of him. His face was slightly aged, bearded, and twisted with overwhelming hate. The Russian was strong, and it took all of Otto's might just to not be thrown off. He tried desperately to close the bolt which the soldier had opened when at the doorway in preparation to shoot; if he could get the barrel over the Soviet, he could shoot him. He soon realised that this was in vain. It seemed that the MP40 had bent the bolt out of place and rendered the weapon useless. Meeting the fearful stare, he tried desperately to find some way to overpower his adversary. This war was not one for dignified combat; Otto spat in the eyes of his Russian opponent, and delivered a headbutt to his nose. Taking advantage of his momentary advantage, he forced the rifle into the chest of the Russian, who took it with him as he hit the wall with a sickening crack and fell to the ground.

It was time to deal with the man still beating Raeder. Otto delivered a harsh kick to the man's ribs, drawing his attention away from Raeder. He tackled Otto with the strength of a bull; if he thought that the first was powerful, this man was a bear. He was grasping at Otto's throat, pinning his arms to prevent any fightback. His breath stank, and he was growling ferociously, dripping saliva across the Tiger driver's face as he continued to starve him of breath. Otto's vision was beginning to tunnel; he had to find a way out soon, or he would never see dawn. Just as he began to lose consciousness, a near-inaudible dull thud could be heard, and the grip on Otto's neck suddenly loosened. The expression on the face of the Soviet had turned to one of surprise, as if he had just awoken and not quite gathered his surroundings. Otto continued to gasp, trying to regain his breath, and understand why the hulking man had ceased his assault. The Russian's eyes lost focus, not diluting as was seen in the face of death, but wildly blinking and straining. Suddenly, the drool which had been dripping on Otto was replaced by a stream of warm blood, which began to flow forward from the back of the head of the victim.

After a few seconds the man slumped onto Otto and turn motionless. The back of the man's head had been caved in, and Raeder was standing behind him with a bloodied shovel and grim expression. He was breathing heavily, and his face was bleeding slightly from the pummelling he had received. Though clearly shaken, Raeder retained his nerve and helped Otto from under the huge carcass of the Russian. For a moment, the two stood in the darkness together, the moonlight providing just enough vision to keep tabs on what had been happening in the fight. The peaceful night was once again torn through by a violent scream, as the Russian Otto had overpowered previously had returned to his feet and was charging the pair, rifle butt aloft with the apparent intention to bludgeon the panzer crewmen.

Otto instinctively threw Raeder out of immediate danger, and prepared to navigate an attempted block against the attack. He hoped to move his arm in the way; the rifle would snap his arm like a twig, but surely better his arm than his face. Just as he braced for the crushing blow, a deafening crack filled his ears, and the aggressor fell to the floor. He had a gaping hole in his abdomen, and could hardly make a noise; Otto looked down on the dying man with overwhelming relief, which was not an emotion he usually felt when so proximate to death. Turning to the tank, he could just about make out the figure of Greim reloading his smoking hunting rifle, with Kellerman and Scholl charging in to provide assistance.

Otto cried out, "Fantastic shot, Herr Hauptman!" before falling to the ground, having become rather faint at the realisation that he had survived such a brush with eternity.

Kellerman and Scholl congratulated Raeder at his quick action, while helping Otto to the Tiger. He could hear a rushing in his ears, and his legs had turned to jelly; he had never, in the whole war, come that close to immediate death. Nor had he been involved in such brutal close quarters combat. Barely able to focus on his surroundings, Otto fell to the ground besides the tank, and simply closed his eyes to sleep, and hoped that this time he would be awoken in calmer circumstances.

His wish was, for once, granted, and he awoke with his face buried in the crisp, dew covered grass. The rain had passed through the fields in the night, and while Otto and the crew had been sheltered under their Zeltbahn material, their surroundings had been almost waterlogged by the downpour. Birds could be heard chirping, and seen duelling across the sky. Otto stretched, arose, and began packing away the cooking station. Greim was already slaving over his maps, as if he did not need sleep. As the crew was preparing to mount the tank and move off, Otto remembered that in the events of the past night he had thrown his MP40 and forgotten to retrieve it. As he strolled towards the cottage, he saw the bodies of the defeated Russians. They were soaked through from the previous night's shower, and drenched in their own blood. It was a terrible sight, these men who had been so full of life only moments ago, turned into inanimate remains.

As he got closer, he realised quite how much the man which had almost killed Otto had bled after Raeder's blow. But the second soldier, shot by Greim, was on his back, yet Otto was sure that when shot, the man had fallen on his front. Then, just as he got within a few metres, the corpse moved. While shocking, the man did not seem to present any threat; his blood had covered the ground around him, and dried into a deep burgundy; his waxy complexion betrayed that he did not have much longer to go. He groaned, gesturing Otto towards him. When he came near and knelt behind the man, he started to speak broken German, in between moans of pain.

"Can you deliver letter for me? Deliver to home, my wife… Tell her, Alexei not afraid… Alexei die well," moaned the Soviet. Otto was almost moved to tears. Granted, this man had tried to kill him only hours before, but could Otto say that he would not act just as ruthlessly if one of his fellow crewmen was in danger? The man could see that Otto was unsure how to answer his command, and chuckled lightly, whispering through gritted teeth. "We both soldiers, no? This war, brings evil. Please, mister, deliver letter." Otto took the blood-stained letter from the trembling pale hand, and placed it in his inner tunic pocket.

The soldier then took out a combat knife, but didn't seem aggressive. He didn't have the strength to attack anyway, and his face was still twisted into a pained smile. He drew in a laboured breath, and asked Otto, "Please, fellow warrior, kill

Alexei. It is okay. I tired of war. Let Alexei sleep now."

Speechless, Otto tried to find a way to talk the man out of such a wish, yet he had seen too many injured men before. He had seen the ghostly white face, the trembling hands, and the pool of blood, and there was nothing that could prevent this man's death. Whether he had minutes, or hours, this soldier had only pain between now and his end. The solider could tell Otto was suffering from internal conflict, and simply hushed him and offered his knife handle. Otto took it, and placed it below the man's throat, allowing the man to observe a few last moments. After about a minute, he gave a brief nod, and the knife was plunged upwards. There was an unusually low amount of blood, with a presumably lowered heartbeat from his steady death across the night. The man briefly jolted, and then settled his eyes, his body stopping all movement. Otto closed the man's eyes, unsure about what he had just done. Was that murder? A favour? Would he hope for equal treatment? What had he done? He had stabbed a dying man; what was one more insane action in this deranged circus of a war?

He didn't have too long to comprehend the morality of this mercy killing, for soon after the man had left this world, artillery had started to thunder down on the fields.

"Griff, get back to the tank! What are you doing, picking flowers? Get a move on!" came the cry from Greim. Every booming explosion was sending a shockwave through Otto's body, with waves of warm air washing over him at increasingly short intervals as the torrent of shellfire grew ever thicker. Springing into action, he dashed the few metres to retrieve his MP40. He began sprinting for the tank, dearly praying that he would avoid any shrapnel. Generally, the Tiger was a safe haven from artillery barrages; while a direct hit might well spell the end for the crew inside, exterior shrapnel – by far the deadliest aspect of long-range shells – would simply bounce from the armour.

Diving back into his driver's seat, he hastily pulled the hatch shut once more. Kellerman jeered at him, hitting him jokily.

"Enjoying the metal rain, were you?" he yelled over the anthem of crashes, while the Soviet guns churned the earth around them into a mess of dirt. Otto was far from the mood for jokes and felt his pocket for the crumpled letter from the Russian.

Before he was questioned for his serious demeanour, Greim issued his order: "Driver, forward."

Chapter 3
97.1 Kilometres From Berlin

The beats of artillery sent shockwaves through the humid crew cabin, as the engine began to rival the explosions for volume. The occasional tapping of the small pieces of shrapnel zipping through the air could be heard as they deflected from the Tiger's hull with a hollow clink.

Greim issued his next command, fighting for his voice to remain audible above the roaring acceleration and squeaking tracks, yelling, "Griff, take us into that village up ahead. We can stop there for fuel, we are running on fumes at this stage!" he said with a gesture to the small settlement which could be seen across the next field.

As they closed the distance from the collection of narrow streets and quaint cottages, the whole crew were searching desperately for some sign of enemy movements. While the odd figure could be made out crossing the roads, they were clad in a multitude of civilian colours rather than Russian uniforms, and walked not with the purpose of a determined attacking soldier, but the dejection of a ravaged population, sick of war. The crew moved slowly and carefully into the village, checking each corner for the dreaded green tank or beige-dressed patrol, yet there were none. Greim had opened his hatch, and hung half out of the turret in order to properly scan the environment, at the great risk of being picked off by one of the Reds' expert marksmen. The inhabitants were the very image of destitution; sullen, hollow faces painted with hunger, torn clothes plagued by soot and brick dust from the countless ruined homes, and the occasional relative searching for their loved ones. Children without parents, lovers without their second halves, and mourners desperately hoping to revive the bodies which littered the tracks; bodies which had been present and lively perhaps only the day previous.

Greim, as always, was keeping his mind focussed on the task ahead, ignoring the misery which surrounded him to inquire with the locals as to the location of enemy forces, and possible sources of fuel. The rest of the crew, however, were speechless. How could their countrymen have been reduced to such an appalling state? How could the victories of 1940 have been turned to ash in only five years? They had been invincible! And yet, they had brought this upon themselves. Their arrogance, their aggression, the entire impetus of the German state since 1933, had failed to bear fruit. Even the stoic Kellerman was almost unable to watch the depiction of pain through which the Tiger walked.

After a few silent stares and crying faces, Greim managed to find a resident who was willing to assist. An old man, who had long cleared sixty years old, informed the crew that the village Gauleiter, or SS representative, had already fled the day before as the Soviets had cleared the area on their way to the Berlin assembly areas.

He continued in a defeated tone, saying, "You'll want to hide that tank, the Russians pass through each midday and evening. My brother has a barn which should do the trick. As for fuel, there are still a few cars whose owners have escaped this war one way or another. You can siphon from them."

Greim thanked him graciously, and Otto moved the Tiger to tail the elderly gentleman to his brother's barn.

An equally ancient man, almost identical but for his walrus moustache and lack of a walking cane, could be seen smoking on a chair outside a great unpainted barn. He expressed absolutely no surprise as the enormous battle-textured panzer emerged into view, and rose shakily from his chair to shake the hand of his brother which had guided the crew here. The men exchanged a mumbled conversation which Otto could not make out from the cabin, which ended with the barn owner rolling his eyes and sighing, before giving a reluctant and grudging nod of his head. The first man signalled Otto onwards, and opened the doors of the barn. Thankfully, the tank just about fit, and Otto reversed through the entrance so as to make a quick escape and issue suppressing shell fire. The crew dismounted as the engine gurgled into silence, and they gathered around their guide.

The old man said to them, "My name is Paul Sichter, and this is my brother Friedrich. We will try to help you while we are here."

Greim, the spokesman of the group, thanked him. "We are grateful of any help you can provide. We are trying to join the Berlin defence," explained the commander. Herr Sichter grunted for them to follow him into the nearest white house, which they entered through the back gate.

"Please, make yourselves at home," announced Paul, taking a seat with a pained groan. "You'll need to be careful. The Gauleiter took every able-bodied man, and indeed some boys, to join the defence when he left a couple days ago. You five will stick out like sore thumbs, not least from your rather distinctive apparel."

Otto glanced about the ragged group and realised that the man was not wrong. They were all dressed in panzer uniforms of a better or worse condition, coated in a mixture of soot, dirt, blood and grease. The smell of the crew, too, when not masked by the fumes of the engine or smoke of fires, was especially pungent in this confined house. The men had all brought their weapons as a force of habit, and could not be more differentiated from the villagers which walked the dusty streets.

"Head upstairs, there are some coats and trousers which you can cover yourselves with. Maybe have a wash too, that stink will be noticed by the Kremlin itself!" mused Paul Sichter.

The group proceeded up the stairs in single fashion, their boots thudding roughly on the clean floorboards, doing their best not to shed mud on the way. Getting to the bedroom, Greim delved into the wardrobe and issued sets of clothes for each on the men. Greim himself couldn't find any to fit his tall frame, and so he remained in his uniform and vowed to stay put in the house. Otto proceeded to the bathroom to wash, and looked into the mirror only to see a totally unrecognisable man stare back at him. Deep purple bags hung under his eyes, and grease smudges littered his face. His neck was bruised from the previous encounter with the Russian scout, and his eyes were devoid of emotion. His hands were caked in dried blood, mud and oil. Using, and largely destroying in the process, the soap of Herr Sichter, he managed to carve something of a recognisable human out of the endemic grime, and changed his tank uniform for the work trousers, grey shirt and brown heavy wool coat provided for him. He adjusted the strap on his MP40 to sit by his side under the coat, should it be required in a pinch, and proceeded out of the bathroom.

Paul had lit a pipe not unlike Kellerman's, and was rocking steadily in his armchair. The rest of the crew, minus Greim, were already dressed and sitting or standing around the room. They all looked rather novel to Otto; Raeder appearing a young farmhand, no outfit change was able to hide the war-rugged face of Kellerman, and Scholl was positively a village priest. Greim and Herr Sichter were sharing a coffee, and Paul's brother Friedrich had started to gather the crew's uniforms to wash in a bowl of water he had prepared outside. Otto handed his garments over with a thankful nod, and took in his surroundings. The house was definitely arranged for two; two comfortable chairs, a double bed, the works. Yet only Herr Sichter lived here, aside from his grandson taken by the Gauleiter, who had a small room downstairs.

Paul told the crew, "Help yourself to my wife's wine. I could never stand the stuff myself," with a shrug, pointing in the direction of a drinks cabinet in the corner.

"Thank you, Herr Sichter, that's very kind," replied Greim with a smile. "But where is Frau Sichter? Surely we should meet her to…" Greim tailed off as he caught sight of something out of the window, over Paul's shoulder. Otto moved to another window to get eyes on what had shocked Greim into silence, but wished he hadn't been so curious. A white sheet lay in the front lawn, covering something strangely body shaped. A red stain was over the front end, dried but not yet old.

Paul sighed deeply and looked outside. "When the Gauleiter came, Monika tried to stop them taking our grandson Stefan. Just fifteen, a boy not ready for war. She begged them, saying that his father was already fighting in the west, and screaming them to cease. I tried to calm her, but she was inconsolable. Then the Gauleiter had had enough. He drew his pistol, struck Monika across the jaw, and shot her." He stared into the middle distance as if he were not in the room, but embedded in a memory. "She just grew still. Stefan was crying as they dragged him away, but I was simply frozen. Fifty-four years, we'd been married. Fifty-four. Never had we ran into such unbridled cruelty. I was just about young enough to serve in the last war, and let me tell you that no one there died for this."

The crew were more than taken aback. How could they know if such a fate had befallen their own friends and relations? Raeder shook his head, and just as he uttered the phrase, "Damned Communists", Paul stomped his foot and clenched his fist.

"Shut up boy!" he snapped, his face burning with anger. "Do you not see that this is what we did to them? Do you not see us reaping what we have sown? We can't take any damned high road! We did this, you fool!"

Raeder muttered an apology, his eyes glued to the floor in shame. The animation left Paul's face, and he sank back into a slouch, grumbling to himself.

A few moments of painful silence passed, until Greim clapped his hands and began to address the crew. "Right, Kellerman, get to work on any repairs and tuning needed on the tank. Raeder, get to town and see if any provisions can be bought, we are nearly out of food. Griff and Scholl, go find that petrol. And all of you, keep a low profile! We can't face an alert until we are ready to move off again," ordered Greim.

The men sprang into action, and Otto and Scholl moved out into the road. Trying not to meet the eyes of the civilians that they passed, they walked to the first car on the opposite side of the street. While they couldn't be sure that the owner had left or indeed been dispatched, the riddling of bullets and explosion-mangled front wheel suggested to the pair that the fuel wouldn't be needed anymore. Scholl began filling the jerry can he had brought, while Otto put his can beside the car and checked continuously up and down the street, sparking a cigarette he didn't even want just to blend better to his surroundings. Scholl spotted his latest tactic to remain covert and stifled a laugh.

"So, you smoke now?" jeered Scholl.

Otto coughed deeply, retorting, "No, Peter, I don't," as he threw the cigarette to the ground, with a chesty cough being broken by a chuckle of his own.

Locals began to stare at the battle-worn faces of the two crewmen, yet no one dared to stop and speak with them. It was roughly midday by now, and the sun beat down against all in the dusty roads. The crew were comfortable enough in their thick coats despite the biting heat, acclimatised as they were to the stuffy conditions of their panzer cabin. After what felt to Otto like an age, Scholl arose from the side of the car with a partially full jerry can in tow.

Turning to Otto, he said, "Why don't you take the next one? I best get this back to the tank," shaking the can to indicate its near full level. Otto rolled his eyes with a smile, and continued down the dirt track which formed the main road of the village.

Arriving at the next car, Otto unscrewed the cap of his jerrycan. The vehicle was, ironically, a German staff vehicle, with SS markings across the side. As he got closer, he could notice the stench of death wafting from the open-topped car. A swarm of flies were darting through the air above the compartment, and a long dead SS officer sat in the rear of the cab, covered in dried bullet holes. His skin had started to rot, with blackened spots peppering his yellowish waxen skin. Otto though it best not to look; it would only be another memory to push out of his mind before he tried to lull himself to sleep each night. Crouching next to the fuel tank, he initiated the siphoning, and heard the container he carried steadily fill up.

By the time the can was roughly half full, a young boy approached Otto. No older that eight, the boy was thin and muddy, clearly hard hit by the recent conflict. His face, however, was not one of malnourished sadness, but of curiosity.

Otto could not evade the boy's observation, and eventually turned to the young man and asked, "Never seen a German soldier, kid?"

The boy chose not to avert his eyes, but simply responded, "Not around here, not in days. What are you doing here? Is the war over?"

Otto smiled, unsure how to answer the question; everything was over, yet carried on. He took a small ration of chocolate he had kept in his trouser pocket and transferred to his civilian attire, and handed it to the boy, in a hope to placate him against asking further difficult questions.

This almost touching moment was interrupted by a loud commotion in the main street, which Otto had turned off of on the way to the wrecked staff car. He could hear some incoherent shouting and yelling, alongside the crashing of breaking wood and the occasional woman's scream. His eyes darted back to the boy in panic; could this be the enemy? The boy gestured hurriedly for Otto follow, and ran to the rear of a whitewashed cottage which backed onto the main street. He took the jerrycan from Otto with visible strain at its weight, and placed it underneath a nearby garden bench, well surrounded with foliage and shrubbery in the untended yard. Otto smiled thankfully at the boy, gave his head a pat and beckoned him to go somewhere safe.

After the boy had returned the way from which the pair had come, Otto made his way down a small path which ran alongside the house and onto the main street. As he cleared the building, he could make out a number of figures buzzing actively across and along the road. The shouts could be identified as Russian, except for one voice; a man stood tall in the centre of the street, in the instantly recognisable blue NKVD cap and trousers, barking clear German inflected with a heavy Soviet accent. His face was one of perpetual cruelty and arrogance. He was yelling his men, of whom there were roughly thirty, to plunder any food, and indeed discarded weapons that could be found among the villagers, while telling the inhabitants that if they had nothing to hide then they had nothing to fear.

Such a security operation was, Otto could only assume, a result of the SS Wehrwulf, or guerrilla unit, activity behind the Russian lines, as the crew had observed themselves in the forest clearing the day before. The crashing of wood he had heard was explicable by Soviet raiders' boots contacting the wooden doors of the village until they broke through, proceeding inside at the protests of those dwelling within. While the odd passer-by was beaten to the ground by a rifle butt, no gunshots had yet rung out, and so the usual murders seemed temporarily on a leash. The Russians had also brought two anti-tank guns into the village, should any German armour make an appearance.

Leaning against the wall of the house he had passed, Otto sighted Scholl crossing the road from the side of the barn and walking towards him. The two men exchanged glances, and began to proceed along the road, attempting to blend by hunching their shoulders and putting their hands in their pockets. Otto himself had brought one arm inside his coat, providing the joint benefit of appearing an invalid soldier and therefore reduced threat, and keeping a firm grip upon his ready cocked MP40 which still hung under the jacket. If he drew the weapon he would surely be killed almost instantly by the surrounding Russians, but it would perhaps help his crew escape through the distraction, and take one or two of the enemies with him, if they were discovered.

As the two trudged along the dirt track, they caught the attention of a Russian soldier standing guard near the road. He moved towards them and began joking with his comrade opposite at the pair's expense. Trying his best to incite either Otto or Scholl to violence, presumably to provide an excuse for killing one or both of them, he refused to let them pass him on the track, and got close to the pairs faces, still jeering with a smirk. After a few moments of Otto desperately biting his tongue, the Russian grew bored with the two. He was, however, evidently frustrated that he had been unable to elicit a reaction from the two men, and so brought his rifle butt sharply into the face of Otto with a thwack, and moved on. Otto was knocked to the ground by the force of the blow; he had trouble regaining visual focus, and felt a small stream of blood run warmly down the side of his head. In his clatter to the floor, he had very nearly fingered the trigger of his concealed machine pistol by accident, and silently thanked God that it had failed to go off.

Scholl helped him to his feet, and the two soldiered on. After a few minutes, the NKVD officer called all his men to the largest and most in-tact house that could be seen, and they ventured inside. Otto and Scholl slipped off into a side lane, and broke into a run as soon as they were hidden from the view of the occupied residence. Wheeling into the garden in which Otto had discarded the jerry can, they sped to retrieve the precious fuel. Hauling the sloshing container from beneath the bench, Otto could feel Scholl staring at him and checking his injury.

"That hurt?" he inquired, gesturing to Otto's broken skin. Otto shook his head, and ran to peak round the corner for any threats. Only one Russian stood guard at the door of the house, with no others visible on the street. "You get moving to the barn. I'll put on a little show for our friend here," smiled Scholl, turning up his collar and ruffling his hair before sauntering over to the Soviet guard.

Seizing his chance, Otto snapped into a sprint. Running as fast as his weary legs could carry him, clinging to the fuel can for dear life and not looking around until he had passed out of sight by at least a dozen metres. Beginning to regain his breath, he moved at still some speed in the direction of the open barn doors. As he unscrewed the cap and began to feed the petrol into the Tiger, he caught the silhouette of Scholl returning from the main road. The bedraggled figure limped towards Otto, with a deep purple bruise across the bridge of his nose becoming visible as he approached.

A small amount of blood seeped from Scholl's nose, and he whispered to Otto, "Those Soviets, they really like hitting people with their rifles, don't they?" Otto patted him on the back and smiled sympathetically, his hand lingering on Scholl's shoulder in a comradely spirit as they both walked back to Herr Sichter's gate and entered the cottage once more.

Paul was still seated where they had left him, only with a broad smile across his bearded face, rather than the sour pout with which he had reacted to Raeder's comment earlier. He and Fritz Greim were exchanging jokes through a cloud of pipe smoke, and laughing merrily. Raeder and Kellerman had returned from repairs to the tank, evident from their hands, which were yet again soiled in grease. Otto and Scholl took a seat by the roaring fire, and had a much-needed rest.

But the faces of the men he had seen die, they haunted him, hanging over his thoughts like a never-ending storm cloud. Their lives, their hopes and wishes, all wiped out. Some as young as boys, they'd had so much to give and tell, yet they were snuffed out in a second. An explosion of a tank shell, the crack of a rifle, and they were gone. But the most disturbing aspect, the image that Otto could never purge from his mind, was the fear. The pure, unbridled, all-consuming terror. The SS man propped against the Panzer in the destroyed column, slowly approaching his end yet not sure when it would finally strike him, desperate to escape the pain yet not ready to leave the world. The Russian tank driver, shocked as he was struck by the round in his back and gasping for air as he sunk into the ground; he had been filled with stories of gloriously serving the Soviet union, emanating the heroes of Stalingrad, yet no one had prepared him for the slow and spluttering death he was enduring as he grew steadily colder and his vision darkened. And brave Alexei, whose letter still sat crumpled in Otto's pocket, transferred from his Wehrmacht uniform before it was washed, had displayed some degree of fright. He was confident, and willing to face whatever fate awaited him, but he could not shake the uncertainty, the apprehension at leaving all he had known. And yet, all of them had left, whether they were prepared or not.

Otto awoke with a jolt and a sharp intake of breath. He had hardly noticed dropping off, and could not tell how long he had been asleep. The scene around him was near identical, but for a few extra empty beer bottles next to Paul's chair. Before the tired driver could fully orientate himself, Paul's brother Friedrich barged through the rear door with a pile of clothes under a sheet.

"Uniforms are washed," he muttered through his moustache, and dumped the items on a table near the centre of the room. Greim thanked the man with a firm handshake and a smile and dished the uniforms out to the men.

"Maybe don't put those on just yet. You could do with a few supplies, no? There is a house, the owner of which won't be requiring use of any of his gathered provisions," informed Herr Sichter. The crew gathered their weapons under their coats once more, and walked out of the door at short intervals; a huge group would be sure to draw the attention of the Soviet occupiers.

Proceeding after Greim, who had asked Paul for the location of the house, they only reduced their spacing as they arrived at the rear door of the indicated house. MP40s drawn, the crew followed Kellerman as he kicked the door from its hinges, and darted about the house to gather sufficient supplies. Sprinting upstairs, Kellerman and Otto ran in the direction of the bathroom, seeking medical supplies, as the rest of the crew scoured the downstairs and pantry. The sounds of their footsteps, however, were soon joined by an increasingly audible set of whispers emerging from the direction of the door opposite what appeared to be the bath suite.

The pair stacked up on the door; Otto's heart was beating out of his chest, his entire body buzzing with adrenaline. His hands and feet were numb, the entire system of his body preparing to face whichever threat was behind the inches of unpainted pine which separated the two crewmen and the mysterious mutters. Kellerman had once again donned his hunter's face, his eyes open wide with focus, and cocked his submachine gun extremely slowly, as to avoid startling the whisper's producer with the sound of internal springs and tumblers. He nodded to Otto to open the door, and, drawing a sharp breath, Otto crashed his boot near the hinges, and as the doorway cleared with a burst of dust and splinters, the pair stormed into the room with MP40s raised.

There was no Soviet contingent, and no ready fighter to meet them. There was simply a huddling mother and daughter, painted with dirt and shivering in fear. Otto, too shocked to act, waited for Kellerman to make the first move, who crouched with the terrified family and reassured them in a calm voice. He handed the little girl his own chocolate ration.

"You don't need to worry about me, sweetie," he said with a smile. "I know I might look scary, but truth is, we are all just as scared as you are!" The girl was still buried in her mother's embrace, but seemed to loosen somewhat, and met Kellerman's eyes with a small smile of her own. The mother thanked him, and Otto went to sit on the bed.

They were soon interrupted. Russian words could be heard, laughed between several individuals downstairs. As boots graced the steps yet again, the mother gestured Otto and

Kellerman into a nearby mostly emptied wardrobe. The pair were not allowed to protest, and hushed as the door was closed, allowing only a crack of light into the cabinet. Otto stared out, hoping to get some idea of the events unfolding in the room. He desperately tried to quieten his breathing, barely able to contain his nerves as the Soviets clattered ever closer.

Two soldiers soon entered the room, armed with Russian submachine guns, not unlike Otto and Kellerman had done only moments before. They joked to each other, pointing at the mother and young girl. As they continued to laugh, they soon began pulling the hair of the mother; Otto prepared his MP40, only too familiar with the rumours of Russian rapes and murders, emanating the German crimes in the wake of Barbarossa. Kellerman eyed him angrily in the darkness, indicating him to hold his nerve and not give away their position. Otto's palms sweated heavily, his knuckles white with the iron grip which he subjected his machine pistol to, and he tried desperately to weigh up the available actions if the Russian chose to try anything that needed stopping.

Thankfully, such actions proved unnecessary. After only pulling the woman's hair and joking to one another, the soldiers left the room, leaving the two civilians otherwise undisturbed. The mother and daughter cried to one another, and Otto carefully swung open the wardrobe door. While Kellerman returned to comforting the shaken pair, Otto proceeded to the window, where he observed the squad of Russians once more retiring from the building. He walked still carefully to the bathroom and began bagging any medical supplies he could find.

Kellerman could be heard asking the girls, "Do you live here? We were told the house was empty." It transpired that the mother and daughter had only been briefly searching the house for supplies and hidden when they heard the tank crew arrive; Paul's intel was correct, therefore, and the men were free to liberate any supplies which they saw fit.

Otto slipped silently down the steps, scanning the room for potential hostiles. While he was fairly confident that he had sighted all the Russians leaving, he could not be certain due to the fact he had failed to ascertain the number which had entered in the first place. He passed through the living room, and began to search the kitchen. A room stripped of all its character, once filled with the sweet scents of home cooking, yet now pungent with stale bread and stagnant dust. Continuing steadily forward, darting his eyes across the room, and listening intently for any disturbance of his surroundings. Muffles upstairs could be identified as Kellerman still consoling the family, yet besides this the area was silent. Otto need listen no further, however, as the air was soon filled with an almighty bang of a storage unit smashing open, and Otto was pinned to the wall by a furious looking man, with a gun barrel pushed into his face.

The man was recognisable as a terrified Raeder, who released Otto as soon as he realised who he was. Apologising profusely, he speedily yelled, "My God! I'm so sorry, Griff! I had no idea it was you! I really didn't!"

Otto simply held up a hand to indicate that Raeder's stuttered apologies had been accepted, and was soon join by Greim, who stepped out from behind a draped curtain, and Scholl, who crawled out from under the sofa. While disappointed at his evidently atrocious room searching skills, Otto was glad to see that his fellow crewmates had been unharmed by the raiding team. Kellerman walked down the stairs and completed the group, who gathered around Greim to receive their next orders.

"That search was pretty much pointless. I can see from Griff's meagre collection that medical supplies were thin on the grounds, and we scarcely found any new provisions at all! I'd say we are done here. Besides, Zhukov's Soviet army have started their renewed offensive, and the defenders around Berlin cannot be expected to hold out for long. It should only take us a day or two to get there, and we must be careful to dodge Konev's Russian tanks approaching from the South," ordered Greim with a wipe to his brow.

The officer was evidently strained with the growing military desperation which faced the Reich he had so long served, despite its moral collapse. Greim had never been a keen National Socialist, but he had been a keen tank commander, and any military man would understandably despair at their flailing armies as they fell from fighting capability. Yet he returned his focus to the moment, and gestured Otto and the crew towards the door through which they had come, following the exhausted men back towards Paul Sichter's residence.

Chapter 4
93.2 Kilometres From Berlin

The team arrived at Herr Sichter's house once more, finding Paul slumped in his chair yet still, greeting their return. They continued into the cottage, and Greim began thanking Paul for his hospitality and explaining that they must now depart the charming village. Scholl indicated to Otto that they should move into the barn and change back into their uniforms, as Kellerman and Raeder proceeded into the bedroom of the cottage to reassume their Wehrmacht attire. Trudging the short distance to their Tiger's shelter, which they had covered with some tarpaulin as to delay detection by a few crucial seconds should anyone glance briefly into the barn, they sighted Paul's brother Friedrich taking a few leisurely sips of a beer stein while sitting on his stool near the barn's entrance. He had been stationed outside to keep an eye out for any overly-curious locals or soldiers, and chosen to fill his watch with intermittent drinking.

Otto and Scholl were soon redressed in their far cleaner uniforms, the stench of sweat and oil being largely swapped for fresh soap, accompanied by a new softness which Otto had not felt for some time. Swinging his MP40 behind him, he waited with Scholl for the arrival of the rest of the crew. But it sounded that Friedrich had arisen from his partial slumber, and was protesting furiously at someone approaching the barn.

"This is outrageous!" he could be heard to cry. "It simply isn't proper; this is my barn!"

The mysterious figure soon barged his way through the small side door through which Otto and Scholl had entered, with a still shouting Friedrich in tow. The man, it seemed, was a young Soviet soldier, no older than his early twenties, displaying a face filled with youthful arrogance.

Otto and Scholl had just enough time to dart behind haybales on either side of the door, and hid in the desperate hope that the Soviet scout would not locate them. They could easily dispatch him with one short burst from their machine pistols, yet this would be at the cost of an immediate compromising of the crew's incognito presence in the village. Friedrich was soon silenced in his red-faced cries by a swift punch to his face that knocked him to the ground, delivered by the Russian as he continued to search the barn. He had not yet sighted the tarpaulin-clad Tiger, largely due to the relative darkness in the barn taking some adjustment to when compared with the bright afternoon sun which beat down outside. But Otto knew that it couldn't be long before it was found, and the alarm raised.

The soldier soon turned in the direction of the covered tank, and his face became twisted with suspicion, as he began to realise just what he was looking at. Otto seized his chance. With the Russian's back turned, the tank driver sprang from his hiding place and wrapped his arms around the man's neck, keeping as tight a grip as he could so as to prevent any scream escaping him. The Russian resisted furiously, desperately trying to shake Otto off and counterattack. Dropping his weight suddenly, Otto forced the pair to the ground, as Scholl jumped from his own hiding place with knife drawn. He dived atop the two already on the floor, stabbing and hacking viciously at the Russian's abdomen. Each slash led to a stronger flailing against Otto's grip, until the Soviet began to weaken as his uniform was coated in red, and the warm blood ran down to stain Otto's clean uniform once more. Eventually, after Scholl had practically carved the poor man into pieces, the resistance stopped and the soldier grew still. Otto cautiously released his clasp, and lay the man's head carefully to the floor.

There was little time to meditate over his actions, as Otto so often did when responsible or even witness to a death. Just as he stood up, the door opened once more, and the rest of the crew entered, followed by a panicked Paul Sichter. Friedrich had also arisen from his punch, and was making his way back to the cottage to tend his split lip. Paul was wringing his hands out of worry and pacing nervously as the crew prepared to remount the Tiger.

"You must hurry!" he cried. "The soldiers, they're coming to check the barn! They had thought their scout would be back by now!" The men climbed into their relevant hatches, except for Greim, who produced an expensive schnapps bottle from his seat and handed it to Herr Sichter with a smile, indicating the gratitude of the crew. Paul grinned at his gift, and stepped back from the tank as its engines revved back to life.

Otto could spy through the crack in the barn's main doors that the contingent of Russians was almost upon them, and prepared to bring the Panzer into action at a moment's notice. Greim closed his hatch, and gave the order to hit full reverse on his signal, negating the effect of any anti-tank weapons which were positioned to ambush them if they left through the main doors. The engine was certainly loud enough to be heard by now, and so stealth was out of the question. The nerves were biting, as Otto waited for the signal to throw the Tiger into action, holding his breath in anticipation.

Just as the doors swung open, allowing light to flood the darkened barn, Otto felt Greim's boot contact his shoulder, and slammed the tank into full reverse. They crashed through the wood at the back of the barn, with splinters being thrown into the air, and the tarpaulin which had coated their machine being thrown off in the wind. The NKVD officer was yelling angrily to his men, and one of the Soviet anti-tank field guns responded by opening fire; due to its being angled to intercept the tank had it jumped forward, however, the shot bounced from the frontal armour with a metallic ring, and shattered into a nearby house with an eruption of brick dust. Paul could be seen visibly cheering at the crew's successful escape, his arms above his head and a great smile on his face. This was until the KGB officer drew his pistol and shot the man dead. Herr Sichter, who had been so accommodating to the men at risk of his own safety, collapsed to the ground with blood spewing from his head.

"I'll kill that bastard!" yelled Scholl, consumed by rage, as he began to rotate the turret towards the officer.

Greim struck the gunner, shouting, "Keep your head, boy! We need to conserve ammunition!" Though even the cool-headed Greim was visibly upset at the abrupt dispatching of their short-lived yet dear friend. The tank continued to reverse quickly, until they had adequate scope to move out of enemy view behind the building to their right. Hollow cracks and bangs could be heard as Soviet troops opened up with small arms fire towards the tank, the shots pinging off insignificantly. Otto brought the Tiger into a sprint, accelerating as quickly as the engine would allow as they wound quickly through the narrow streets which could barely accommodate the tank. Raeder laid down suppressive fire on the main road which was visible at the end of the snicket down which they travelled, occasionally striking the odd soldier which darted across the gap, throwing them to the floor, motionless.

Finally, the Tiger arrived at the T-junction which joined them onto the main road of the village, along which they would have to travel some fifty metres, before turning off once more to escape to the haven of the forest onto which the village bordered. The high street was almost certainly guarded by the anti-tank guns which the crew had noticed earlier, ready to blast the tank as it broke out from the sideroad. Otto slammed the brakes as they approached the opening, allowing only the first couple feet of the Tiger to become visible from either side of the road. This was a trick he had picked up back when the army had the capacity to actually attack occupied areas; many jumpy gun crews would loose their shells prematurely as they saw the tank hove into view, either missing or causing hopefully minimal damage. Sure enough, two explosions thundered off the walls of the cottages, as shells zipped past the tank inches from Otto's drivers' sight. Taking the opportunity of their reload, the tank wheeled to the right as it moved through the entrance, and the team hurried to acquire their targets before they were visited by yet more fire.

The street was emptied of civilians, who had run into their homes at the first gunshots, leaving little risk of stray shots finding innocent flesh. The Russian guns could be seen at the end of the street, about a hundred metres from their position. The machine guns were peppering the gun crews, soon emptying the first, but the second managed to get a shot off. A fantastically lucky shot from the tank's constantly firing machine guns managed to hit the shell on route, exploding it mid-air and showering the tank in thick, but not quite penetrating, pieces of casing. Their good fortune was near unbelievable; it seemed that the Russians were using high explosives, at the hope of knocking out the Tiger's tracks and to capture it with their infantry. They were certain not to survive another shot like that, and were just short of the path down which they had to travel.

The following moments were as if in slow motion. Greim yelled at Scholl to fire into a house on the right, the same house which the team had looted for supplies, and lay just beyond their designated turn point. He also commanded Kellerman to load a high explosive shell on a delayed fuse, one of only two remaining. Finally, he shouted that Scholl should fire as low into the houses walls that he could, and to shoot as soon as ready. The crew followed his instructions without question, so desperate was the situation that they simply trusted Greim's instincts to get them out alive. A boom signalled that the shell had been sent, flying from the turret at tremendous speed.

The fruits of Greim's quick thinking were instantly apparent. The shell crashed through the house's wall, but failed to over-penetrate through the other side due to the low area at which it had been fired, and rather struck the floor on the other side. Nor did it explode instantly at contact, due to the delayed fuse, but rather waited half of a second, causing the energy to be directed outwards from within the house itself. This precipitated a huge shower of dust and debris to be strewn across the street in a spectacular fashion, as almost the entire structure disintegrated in front of them. Dust billowed upwards, completely blocking the tank from the view of the gunners. Greim kicked Otto, who could only assume that he should turn left in order to provide the steep angle for any incoming shells and minimise penetration. As planned, the first projectile was incorrectly aimed on account of the smoke, and hit the Tiger at such an angle that it was sent well behind the village. The second, fired from the other gun which had evidently been re-manned by Soviet troops, clattered into the still falling masses of debris with a bang, releasing an orange glow into the dust. By the time that the gunners had time to chamber a third round, the tank had whizzed round the corner into the side street, and was prancing towards the forest.

Many in the cabin audibly cheered and laughed, so glad were they to have gotten out of such an impossibly tight spot. Even the stony-faced Kellerman let out a triumphant roar at the close-cut escape. Raeder opened his eyes again, so expectant had he been of the crew's demise, and was nearly moved to tears when he found that the tank – and indeed, he – was still whole.

Otto still felt shaken by the death of Herr Sichter, yet suddenly realised that there may have been more dead innocents, shouting, "What about the mother and daughter in that house?" But Kellerman reassured him that he had made sure that they got out safely while Otto was searching downstairs.

The crew stopped when safe into the forest, and angled the gun in the direction from whence they'd came. The Russians, however, had failed to follow them, possibly bracing for a perceived counterattack, or simply not of sufficient strength in either men or materiel to be able to hunt the Tiger. Raeder hopped down from the tank to make a quick inspection of the hits upon their machine, while the rest of the crew took a much-needed breather. Kellerman's triumphant smile had been replaced by an expression even more grave than usual.

"I used to serve in anti-partisan units. I've seen what we used to do to collaborating villages. I can only hope that the Reds won't follow our lead," he said to the crew in a depressed tone. Otto simply offered him a pat on the shoulder, and tried to stay focussed on the task at hand.

"Hurry up, boy," moaned Kellerman, wanting Raeder to finish up and get back in the tank. Moments later, a panting Raeder jumped into his seat.

"Only minor damage, Herr Hauptman," he told Greim while reloading his MG34. Otto once again increased the fuel being pushed through the Tiger, and began to move forward. The road to Berlin was littered with small wooded thickets such as this, usually little more than a few miles in depth, from which the tank could hop between as cover. Raeder soon noticed that he had loaded his last ammunition box, and indicated to the crew that, if they could find any, it would be worth picking up.

Before long, a small group of field-grey and green clad individuals emerged from the bushes ahead of the Panzer. They seemed unalarmed, and when the crew got closer, it became clear that they were German soldiers. Yet 'soldiers' was a generous term indeed. Boys and old men. Greim appeared from his hatch and began talking to the group leader, a short middle-aged SS man with a tiny temper. He was constantly followed by three burly-looking troops, who maintained the appearance of seasoned veterans; such an appearance was also greatly amplified by the comparative weakness displayed by their comrades.

The men were exhausted. Their faces were covered with mud, yet their eyes were still clearly bagged. Their faces gave one simple message, passed by almost every method except speech: "We give up." They were ripped from their homes and simply waiting for this war to finish. Their weapons, too, were highly outdated; largely armed with Gewehr 98's from the First World War, and the odd extremely young lad was simply carrying ammunition. This was excepting the SS bodyguards, who carried Sturmgewehrs and Panzerfausts. It seemed to Otto that this rag-tag group was a perfect metaphor for the German military situation at large, or even the state of the entire nation. Broken and dying.

It soon transpired, according to Greim's conversation with the men, that their leader was the infamous Gauleiter who had been terrorising the village of Herr Sichter, and taken the settlement's sons for combat service. Paul's grandson Stefan, for whom Monika Sichter had died, should also be here, therefore. While furious at the Gauleiter's actions towards the villagers, Greim thought it pertinent to contain his rage until they could learn the location of Stefan. Eventually, the SS official barked an order, and a young boy stepped forward from the group.

He was bedraggled even by the standards of his fellow conscripts. His face wore an expression laced with pain and destitution, hurt by the loss of his grandmother and the days of hell which had ensued. The young boy's body, too, displayed the marks of war, with bruises and lacerations decorating his exposed arms and face. His blonde hair was interwoven with mud and soot, and his blue eyes washed out by nights of restlessness. It seemed strange that the 'ideal Aryan' had been so ground down, despite all the pointless propaganda. Stefan stepped towards the Tiger and looked up at Greim.

"You're Stefan Sichter?" inquired the tank commander, looking down sympathetically at the beaten soldier.

"Yes, sir, that I am. What's this all about, sir?" he asked, with a sense of anticipation in his voice, perhaps hoping for a liberation from this nightmare.

Greim took a deep breath, and eyed the young man with respect, telling him, "Your grandfather and grandmother were good people. She tried to stop you leaving, and he was extremely brave and accommodating by helping us find fuel and food. You should be very proud."

Stefan could be seen to almost well up at the memory of Monika Sichter's murder and could tell by Greim's tone and use of past tense that some fate had befallen Paul also. At this point the SS leader regained an interest in the conversation, turned from the chat he had been having with his cronies, and barked an order for Stefan to return to his position.

"What the hell is this all about? First you ask to see one of my men without cause, then you fill him with paltry sentiment?" the man yelled, his face growing red with the strain. Greim maintained a cool and calm expression, yet Otto could see under the turret hatch that he was cocking his Luger pistol, and so the crew followed suit by covertly readying their MP40s.

"You're the man that shot Monika Sichter?" asked Greim calmly, not allowing his hate to bubble out in his voice.

The leader let out a guttural laugh, saying, "What, that pathetic bitch? She had it coming! Interfering with SS business like that!" The crew were, by now, physically restraining themselves from obliterating the SS officer in a hail of bullets.

Greim continued his questioning, asking the man, "What

is it you'll be assigning them to, then? These boys?"

The officer lent forward, and in a quietened tone, revealed that the plan was to send the soldiers in a suicidal counterattack at the village, to possibly disrupt Soviet advances. This was indeed suicide; there were no more than fifteen men, facing two-to-one in numbers as they attacked the fortified village beset with battle-hardened, well-armed Soviets. The SS officials' tents were still set up, suggesting that they would not in fact be joining the young men on the march, but simply complete their own retreat to Berlin.

Greim shrugged and smiled at the ridiculousness of the plan put before him. Before the SS officer had time to react, Greim raised his pistol and landed two shots squarely into the man's chest, killing him instantly. The next moments were like a blur. The young boys simply ran to cover, so unacquainted were they with the sounds of battle. The three bodyguards, however, had sprung into action. Kellerman managed to jump out of his hatch and mow one of them down with a machine pistol burst before the soldier had the chance to draw his rifle. The other two had begun to return fire, however, with their suppression forcing the crew to duck back beneath their hatches.

Kellerman had been grazed by a bullet before he had managed to hide behind the Tiger's armour, but yelled reassurance to the crew that he was all right and it had only been a flesh wound. Awaiting a break in the fire, Otto prepared to jump up and take one of the men out in their reload. He sprung from his seat and fired wildly into the bushes behind which one of the men had ran, eventually hearing a yell and experiencing no returned shots. Finally, the crew arose cautiously from their hatches, looking across the bushes and treeline for the third and final opponent. Otto had expended his ammunition spraying the shrubbery, and was searching the cabin for his spare magazine.

The forest was silent with anticipation. The blowing of the trees could be heard mixing with the trembling breaths of the crew, who knew that the next moment could well be the end. No footsteps, no sounds of equipment. Suddenly the man emerged from behind the Tiger with Panzerfaust readied. While the hollow charge of the Panzerfaust might not be guaranteed to pierce the Tiger's armour, it was far from impossible, and not a dice that the crew were willing to roll. Greim, the only crewman in view of the assailant, went to dispatch him with his Luger, yet cursed as the weapon jammed with a disappointing click. With Greim fumbling with the action, it seemed that the soldier would be allowed to release the rocket into the helpless tank.

The next sound to greet the ears of the combatants was the crack of a rifle shot, rather than the woosh of an anti-tank projectile. The SS soldier dropped his weapon, clutching desperately at his chest and stumbling backwards. A second shot hit his gut, and he fell to the ground, writhing briefly before turning still. The crew looked around in wild confusion as to where their saviour stand, who had delivered such well-aimed shots. They could make out a figure standing near where the young men had run at the outbreak of the firefight.

Stefan stood with his rifle still smoking, staring at the felled soldier. His weapon was levelled perfectly, and he waited to see that the man had turned to corpse before cycling the spent brass casing from the chamber of his Gewehr. He lowered the stock from his cheek to reveal a face of intense focus, not dissimilar from Kellerman's huntsman gaze, rather than the wide-eyed fear that adorned the faces of his comrades. The shots, too, had been well aimed and delivered from well over fifty metres at a standing stance. These were the hallmarks of a veteran soldier, which was only dispelled when Stefan then realised what he had done and started to look rather shaken at the prospect.

Greim was visibly impressed at the young man's marksmanship, while the rest of the crew including Otto chose to focus on the fact that they had not been fried by the Panzerfaust warhead. Gesturing the boy to come back towards the tank, Greim smiled in praise and asked the shaken soldier, "Where did you learn to shoot like that, boy?"

Stefan seemed upset, saying, "My grandfather, Herr Paul Sichter. He used to take me out with his old war rifle and teach me to hunt. This rifle is his; he handed it to me when they dragged me away. He said it could keep me safe. I've practiced with it for as long as I can remember."

Otto reckoned that Stefan would cry if only he had the energy or fluids to do so, but he simply stood, unsure what to do next.

"Boys!" yelled Greim, addressing the young men the Gauleiter had gathered. "We need you to do one more thing for us. Check these bodies for anything which might help us, such as ammunition, or intelligence on Soviet positions."

With that, the Hauptman sat back down in his commander's seat, with the crew following. Had they just killed fellow Germans? There was sure to be a court martial for such a crime. Otto noticed, however, that he didn't feel the same level of guilt that he had done when he had taken lives previously. Even Alexei, a nominal enemy who had gone to his end with relative bravery and acceptance, had caused Otto enormous pangs of regret and horror when compared with his direct role in the death of these SS individuals.

Eventually, one of the young soldiers returned to the tank with a piece of paper aloft, also holding a bandage and two MP40 magazines. Greim, who had by now unjammed his pistol and returned it to holster, took the supplies and studied the documents. He told the crew that the intelligence report claimed the German defences around Berlin were on the verge of collapse, and preparing to withdraw into urban defence within the city itself. After such a point it would be impossible for any forces to worm their way through the Soviet line. It would also be necessary for the crew to make radio contact with the defenders, in order to call a local counterattack and get their tank into the defensive network. While it would be bold to prevail upon such an action, the necessity of a further tank in the defence line, let alone a powerful Tiger, might convince the ground troops to break a hole through which they could slip.

After the documents had been memorised, Greim called forward Stefan once more. The boy had stopped reeling from his baptism of fire, and he now searched for purpose and a plan. Greim dismounted the Tiger, and looked the dejected soldier in the eye, issuing his next orders. "You have a fine nerve, and keen shot. Most of these soldiers which you call your comrades are children and old men, and so you shouldn't let your age hinder your potential. But you must lead them now." Greim unpinned his own Iron Cross, still leaving the Knight's Cross around his neck, and fastened it to the uniform of Stefan. "I present you, Stefan Sichter, with the Iron Cross first class in the name of your own bravery and that of your grandparents. I can think of few so deserving recipients. Now you keep these men safe, it is a lot of responsibility! It is your choice whether you go with them to a warrior's death, or simply return to your homes. And whatever way this war goes, you can tell the powers that be that Hauptman Fritz Greim assigned your award, and you cannot therefore be blamed for any suggestions that it was undeserved."

The boy did not say a word. He simply smiled gratefully, shook Greim by the hand, and returned to his new subordinates. Greim clambered back onto the tank, and now addressed his own crew, who were clearly unnerved at their killing of fellow Germans.

"You are clearly conflicted," he told the crew in a paternal tone. "But those men who we killed today; they were not warriors. A warrior does not prey upon the innocent, they do not commit such heinous crimes as those inflicted upon the village. Make no mistake, these SS men are just as much a threat to Germany as the Soviets or British, and even more your enemy. The Russians may be brutal, but the majority of them deserve the title 'soldier'. So, don't let it stress you men, as best you're able to, for our victims today were not Germans, but monsters. Onwards, Griff."

Otto began moving the Tiger slowly forwards, but Greim's short speech had really chimed with him. Perhaps this was why he did not feel regret at their deaths. Maybe these criminals had put themselves beyond redemption, and as their world collapsed around them, only yet more moral waste could ensue. Their reality was dying, these SS butchers, and they were willing to do whatever they could to keep their power, and indeed selves, alive.

The most dangerous creature was always a desperate one.

Chapter 5
81.8 Kilometres From Berlin

There was a strange dichotomy to the country through which the Tiger traversed. Otto could look in one direction to see a picturesque landscape, with forests standing tall against ploughed fields, which were dotted with quaint cottages. Yet in the other direction lay the endemic scars of war, the conflict having ripped through the earth and skies, leaving flaming wrecks and choking smoke stacks in its wake. It always struck him as surreal, how these two absolute opposites were so interwoven across his home nation, increasingly mixed as they approached Berlin, until the war would ultimately conquer and eliminate nature, creating hell on earth.

It always seemed a delicate balance to Otto, how the war interplayed with its surroundings, being more or less dominating of the environment the closer they travelled to the front. The evening sun was by now almost masked by the treetops, with the orange and purple light painted across the patchily clouded sky. The sun was stunning to the crew as it passed through their view slots, casting a lengthy shadow behind the rumbling tank. The searchlights were starting to shoot across the air of Berlin once more, reflecting from the ever-present black smoke of the Russian bombardment. The anti-air weapons, too, were throwing tracers into the sky against a swarm of Soviet bombers, which were steadily approaching the area. The aircraft were speckled by the constant black dots of flak, and sometimes ducked out of the formation and began to hurtle towards the floor, with a trail of darkened fuel and smoke at their tail. Occasionally, an aircraft would burst into a tremendous display of golden orange flame, as either the bomb bay or oil store was ignited.

The sounds of battle were distant still, yet becoming ever more audible. Dull cracks of rifle shots and patters of machine guns could be heard alongside the deeper booms of explosions and armoured fire. A quiet drone of bombers could also just about be made out whenever Otto opened his hatch to alleviate the heat. This was all fighting to be noticed above the harsh revs of their Panzer's engine, which was able to move quicker with the fuel plundered from the village. The men still had a number of items to source before they could break into Berlin, however; they needed to establish radio contact with the defenders, and ideally find spare 7.92 millimetre ammunition for Raeder's bow-mounted machine gun. Finally, the crew would have to be sparing with their shells, which ran dangerously low at eight, and two smoke rounds.

The crew soon noticed, however, a disturbance in the skies. A fighter had peeled off from the main formation, and was approaching their position at some speed, with two metallic specks in tow. As it approached, the yellow nose and pale blue undercarriage informed the crew that it was in fact a German fighter, a rare sight indeed in these past months. The Luftwaffe had been facing mounting losses under the weight of the Soviet Air Force, which had ground down its number of aircraft in a battle of attrition which Germany simply couldn't keep up with. Indeed, the reduced number of fighters led to their being committed in ever fewer numbers, which in turn increased their chance of destruction as they were fed to the enemy piecemeal.

The fighter continued to roar in the direction of the Tiger, yet it didn't seem to be aiming for the crew; it was more likely, thought Otto, that it had simply darted in this direction by chance after coming under fire. The pursuing aircraft looked to be Yak fighters, and they were hurling streams of tracer bullets through the sky which the German pilot was working desperately to avoid. His engine was spluttering and cutting out intermittently, with the chronic fuel shortage which plagued the German forces leading his aircraft to have been insufficiently supplied with petrol. To worsen matters, his wing had been pierced and a black liquid was spraying from his aircraft due to a ruptured tank.

The fighter was unable to maintain its altitude at such pitiful throttle, and the Soviet planes were closing in. After a few more evasive swerves, the fighter, which Otto could now see to be a Messerschmitt Bf-109 E-3, was clipped rather badly by one of the machine gun bursts. The fuel leak evolved into a tail of fire, following the aircraft as it descended still lower to the ground. The flying machines now passed over the top of the crew's tank, clearing the turret by only perhaps thirty feet. Hot oil from the fighter spattered the Tiger, releasing the potent stench of petrol into Otto's nose far more strongly than the Panzer's ambient engine odour.

The Luftwaffe pilot had lowered his flaps, and seemed to be aiming to ditch his aircraft in the field through a belly landing. The Yaks were still close on his tail however, and while one maintained the pressure of tailing the Messerschmitt, the other Soviet pilot broke off high, using his superior speed and greater fuel usage to invert and dive down upon the slow-moving German. A final second-long burst delivered from almost directly above the German fighter caused his aircraft to suddenly dip. Otto was by now squinting to observe events which were unfolding hundreds of metres away, but it seemed that the German had abandoned his careful controlled descent at the Russian's last burst, and the nose of the aircraft plunged sharply into the dirt. An amount of debris snapped from the aircraft, which had kicked up a thick brown dust cloud, and finally the plane came to a halt.

    Greim issued the order for Otto to halt the Panzer and begin travelling to the aircraft, which had crashed just shy of a kilometre to the left of the Tiger, in an open field much like the one in which the tank currently stood. Otto swiftly obeyed; it seemed unlikely to him that the pilot would have survived such a horrendous crash, but it was surely the duty of the crew to provide assistance if he had. The triumphant Yaks were doubling back towards their bomber formation now; one fighter, however, had spotted the Tiger, and thought it advantageous to loose a short burst of cannon fire in the direction of Otto and the crew. The rounds bounced merrily from the Tiger's armour, and while the comparatively inexperienced and nervous Raeder flinched and winced at every ping, the more hardened crew did not even react to such a trifling attack, so trusting were they of the metal which separated them from the outside world.

    The crackling flames grew louder as they approached the wreck. Otto could smell the burning engine oil, and had to hold a handkerchief over his face in order to avoid choking on the thick, billowing smoke. The field, too, had been terribly marked by the landing of the plane; sprouting wheat had been torn up by the huge drag marks left by the aircraft, being replaced by a muddy trench where the plane had skidded heavily across the ground. The propeller had bent inwards with the impact, and one of the wings had partially broken from the fuselage. It was, all things considered, a less than encouraging image for the crew checking for any living pilot.

Otto and Raeder dismounted their Panzer and ran towards the crumpled fighter. The Yak aircraft were, by now, elevating steadily to re-join their escort, and unlikely to cause any more trouble for the Tiger crew. They could see the still figure of the pilot silhouetted against the glass of the cockpit, which they soon realised had been coated with crimson. The aircraft had been riddled with puncture holes, and it appeared that the cockpit had not escaped such punishment; the glass had been cracked and shattered by the final Soviet burst of bullets. This explained the disappearance of the pilot's masterful handling of the decent; he had been shot several times in the final strafe, and likely killed instantly.

"I have to say, Otto, I don't fancy his chances," mumbled Raeder, desperation tinging his voice.

"Perhaps you are right, he certainly doesn't seem to be attempting any escape from his burning aircraft," sighed Otto, adding, "but we might just extract some ammo for your MG before it goes up?"

Raeder's face filled with recognition at the opportunity that this wreck provided to get his weapon back into use, and called for Kellerman at the top of his voice. The aged engineer sprinted towards the pair, automatically bringing a small toolkit; why else would Raeder have called? Otto told Kellerman about their need to extract the aircraft ammunition, and he swiftly set to work, hammering, plying and unscrewing several plates and components to expose the bullet storage. He,

Otto and Raeder gathered all the belt sections which they could carry, and hurried back to the tank.

They had finished just in time. At the moment Otto climbed back onto the tank, which had been parked a few dozen yards from the downed plane, he was rocked by a thunderous boom and engulfed in a wave of warm air. The fire had spread to the fuel supply, and caused an eruption of flames. The pilot could just be seen through the smoke, roasting in the wreck of his defeated fighter. The fuselage was cracking and breaking in the heat, sounding lesser bangs through the orange glow of the fire. Turning back to their vehicle, the crew remounted their Tiger and closed hatches.

Greim addressed his men as to their next objective. "We need to get hold of a functioning radio. The Berlin defenders can still, just about, launch extremely local counterattacks, and we will need them to help us break in and pass those determined Reds, rather desperately I should think!"

Raeder had been attempting to re-wire the Tiger's own damaged radio for some days now, with no luck as yet. "I think I can raise our own stations on a Soviet radio, but it'll need to be better than those in their tanks. Something wonderfully high tech will do, like a command station or forward headquarters," reported Raeder, with a palpable sense of nervousness at the prospect of attacking such a fortified position.

Beset with concentration, Greim was desperately studying his map and the gathered SS documents to find an answer to the predicament in which the crew found themselves. After some time, he looked up in triumph.

"There seems to be a Soviet divisional headquarters somewhere here," informed Greim while pointing at a wide area of the map a few miles from Berlin's outskirts.

"Where exactly, though, Herr Hauptman? We are going to need some better intelligence of the area before we attack," replied Otto. Simply roaming the general location in which they believed a base lie was no plan at all, and Greim knew it.

"Naturally, Gefreiter Griff. We will use this small forest for cover," replied Gerim with a gesture towards a green patch on the map. "And we will intercept a scouting party. Most Soviet command centres, even small ones have armoured patrols covering the nearby regions. If we can capture one of their tanks while not raising the alarm, they might have maps or tips as to what awaits us in their base."

Wooded pockets were proving to be the salvation of the Tiger and its crew in these final days. They provided quick and easy camouflage, and shelter from enemy air attack, while remaining simple to escape. Many forests were spaced out and able to be moved through, as well as crossed with roads, and the tank could overcome many of the smaller trees and shrubs. Yet again, the machine was rolling through the fields bound for a collection of trees, though this time it was in preparation for a rare offensive.

It was twilight by now. The landscape grew dark, with just enough light to show the crew what lay in front of them. Shadows lay long across the terrain, and the chirping birds were beginning to adopt their evening silence. Eventually, the tank's brakes ground the metallic hulk to a halt, just inside the wooded enclave to which Greim had directed the crew. Now all that remained was the near herculean task of actually finding and capturing a Russian tank, all without raising the alarm of the nearby base!

The Panzer crew racked their brains for any available methods to seize a tank in relative stealth. Small arms fire, and even grenades, would be applicable in their assault, due to their comparatively high-pitched sound signature being unlikely to travel to the Soviet base. The principal weapon usually available to the crew, however, was their Tiger's 105 millimetre bite, and the thunderous boom which it released was absolutely out of the question for any low-profile attack. It was also necessary that the tank they assaulted did not fire its own piece, for the same reasons. It followed, therefore, that the crew would be required to assault and capture a hostile tank on foot, and all before it was able to aim and fire its main gun. This bordered on the impossible.

Auditing their weapons, the men could muster an MP40 each, save Greim who was restricted to his hunting rifle and pistol. On the other hand, the crew enjoyed an abundance of stick grenades. Kellerman had always ensured that they maintained a plentiful supply, not least by virtue of the device's usefulness in assaulting damaged tanks, as proven earlier in the forest clearing. Over the years he had built quite a stash, and now boasted over fifteen such grenades. Kellerman had already set to work by his own initiative, bundling some of the charges to create an anti-tank grenade. This was likely to at least liberate a T-34 or any smaller tank of its track, immobilising the target.

Otto, Scholl, and Raeder had dismounted the Panzer and were beginning to adorn their uniforms with leaves, grass and branches from the forest floor, coating their exposed faces and hands with mud to blend better with their surroundings. In order to successfully assault enemy armour on foot, speed was critical; much like a leopard or cheetah in the wild, they had to remain undetected until they had closed the gap between themselves and their target as much as possible, making the pounce all the quicker to overcome. When they had stalked as close as they dare to their prey, the anti-tank bundle would be used to disable the Soviet machine, and the crew would then have to charge the enemy and work out how to evacuate its occupants before they were able to summon assistance.

"Griff, Raeder and Scholl, you will cover Kellerman as he places the grenade. I will remain in a position to provide sniper assistance, should you be caught short," ordered Greim. "Try to keep gunfire to a minimum. Complete silence is not necessary, and the odd burst should simply blend in with the ambient crackling of battle. Do not, however, allow any nearby Soviet units believe that there is any sort of substantial firefight underway for which they should provide help."

"Yes, Herr Hauptman," replied Otto. It was imperative that the crew did not alert other scouts; two tanks would be far more than the dismounted men could handle.

Eventually, Otto and his comrades were ready. Having hidden their Tiger amidst the shrubbery, they began to venture towards the nearest road. They had no idea where to locate a Soviet patrol tank, but any well-used thoroughfare seemed a good place to start. Trudging through the soft spring mud, it struck Otto that he had almost spent as much time out of his tank than inside it these past few days. For the majority of his military service, he had spent long hours in the stuffy crew cabin, days at a time of only dismounting to sleep, and even then, only when circumstances allowed such luxury. Yet now that his mighty Tiger was without infantry support, or indeed fellow armour, it was rendered strangely vulnerable. The crew had often neglected the importance of their foot-bound counterparts, rocketing ahead of the advance to challenge Russian tanks alone, and yet such support was now sorely missed.

When the Red counterattack had cut Otto's Panzer from fellow Wehrmacht personnel, and the Berlin defence line, they had been reduced from a metallic alpha predator, unchallenged except by some of the largest Soviet machines, to that of a scavenger, darting from forest to forest in hope of shelter. In fact, the only reason that the Russians had failed to wipe out their own Tiger was its hidden position in a small wood while guarding a road. The shattered SS Panzer column, from which the crew had scavenged ammunition earlier, demonstrated the fate which could well have faced Otto and his crew at the hands of the Red steel tide. They strived to reach the Berlin line, despite the fact that the war's outcome was by now a foregone conclusion; the crew were more searching for a sense of normality and certainty which they craved, a feeling of which they had been deprived since being separated from their formation days earlier. This was, Otto figured, why it was so necessary to the crew to not consider why they fought on, for any logic in doing so was inherently flawed. Simply carry on.

In the steadily dying light, Otto's thoughts were interrupted by Greim. "Here, a light tank has passed through recently enough," he observed.

Greim's aptitude for hunting had made him an expert tracker, and so locating the movements of something as overt as a tank was no challenge. When Otto arrived at where the commander was crouched, he could make out two tracks which lay closer together than their own Tiger, or even a T-34. Fritz Greim was sniffing the soil and feeling for the tracks, likely ascertaining the recency of their producer. Suddenly the commander stood, confident in his findings, and began issuing his plans to the men. "We will ambush it when it comes back through. It shouldn't be too long; Soviet scouts are fast, and its route is likely short. Conceal yourselves, men!"

The wait was longer that Otto had hoped for. The men hid in the foliage for over half an hour, seeing off the rest of the evening's sunlight. The night was nearly pitch black, only relieved by the strength of the full moon, the light from which seeped through the treetops of the forest. The crew could just about gather their surroundings, having adjusted to the darkness, though the information imparted by their eyes was far from clear. Crickets littered the forest floor, providing a subtle song to which the crew listened. The anticipation of the enemy tank was being steadily replaced by sheer boredom, the men laying hidden increasingly desperate for something to happen, if only to break their monotony.

Kellerman lay next to Otto, struggling to stay awake. Isaac Kellerman was possibly the crew member most born of war. He had the greatest concentration and performance imaginable when in the fires of combat, yet when he was not under threat of death he almost seemed to vegetate. The man could not be said to enjoy war, far from it; he could often be heard mourning the loss of his son, and vocalising the absurdity of this conflict. He did, however, seem to come to life when under fire, as if he had become so acclimatised to danger that it was the only field in which he could now thrive. Otto had seen such symptoms in many fellow soldiers, though in Kellerman it was particularly pronounced. Otto feared that the poor shell loader would never again adjust to civilian life.

One tedious wait later, and the near-silence of the darkened environment was broken by the hum of a distant engine. It was revving quickly, and as the sound grew closer, the steady clacking of its tracks could be heard. Looking down the forest path, Otto spied the moonlight which passed through the trees glinting off of a metal hull, steadily rolling across the ground. It was hard to see any details through the gloom, but he could just about ascertain that the enemy tank was small, smaller than a T-34, perhaps a BT-5? These compact machines, once the mainstay of Soviet armour, were now relegated to scouting duty, due to both their speed and relative combat uselessness when compared with their larger German and Russian counterparts.

The tank was perhaps a minute from being upon them, and so the men readied themselves. They would not be spotted by the enemy crew until the attack; the shadows were serving the crew well, buried under their bushes. Greim had retreated to a sniping position which provided a better view of the road. It was easy to mistake Greim's usual distance from the action for cowardice, yet each of the crew were fully aware that this was nonsense; the commander would happily throw himself into danger in the place of any of his men, yet was cursed to be the sharpest shot in the team, and so his best deployment was often further from the enemy. He had also undertaken rudimentary training in all of the crew's positions, and so could replace any one of them should the need arise.

As the hulk rumbled closer, the mud on which Otto lay began to tremble and vibrate to its engine. Kellerman unscrewed the priming charge on his anti-tank grenade bundle, preparing to fling the weapon under the enemy's tracks. It would be vital to move out of the shrapnel's path as soon as the explosive was deployed, diving either onto the tank or behind it. Otto readied his weapon, and took a deep breath in anticipation. He could see the prone figures of Scholl and Raeder preparing themselves on the other side of the road,

Scholl trying desperately to comfort Raeder and steady his nerve. Otto himself felt almost sick with fear as the tank neared him, his legs numb and his heart in his throat. Kellerman had reassumed his combat focus, and the pair waited for the right moment to attack. They would give anything to regain the boredom of a few moments previously.

Kellerman patted Otto, and the men jumped up from their hiding positions. Otto's mind was only focussed on one word: move. He sprinted without thinking of his feet, running as if floating as he closed the distance to his kill. Kellerman pulled the pin from his device and hurled it under the nearest track, leaping onto the side of the tank to avoid the blast. Whispered Russian confusion could be heard from inside the tank, as the German pirates climbed aboard. Otto got to the tank, diving into the soft mud behind it with a squelch, and desperately hoping that the Soviet driver did not choose to reverse and spell his end. He held his hands over his head, and prayed that the stray shrapnel would avoid him.

An almighty sharp prang erupted into the night air, causing Otto's ears to ring. The Soviet tank continued for a moment, then rattled to a halt as it became clear that the track had been thrown. The whispers inside the cabin had arisen into panicked yells, as the inhabitants struggled to grasp the unfolding situation. Otto hurried to his feet once more, and sheltered at the side of the tank. The crew all stayed as close to the machine as possible, in order to render its turret ineffective against such close-range targets. The main gun was rotating wildly, trying to find targets among the shadows by which it was surrounded.

Eventually, the turret stopped swinging, as the tank's occupiers realised that their tormentors were actually on top of and around their machine. Otto, Scholl, Kellerman and Raeder now exchanged glances, each hoping that the other would bring forward a solution for eliminating or drawing out the enemy crew. The usual grenade-clearing was invalid, for fear of any essential intelligence or maps which might assist their assault on the command centre being destroyed in the blast. This was an unusual Mexican standoff; if Otto and his comrades opened the Soviet hatch first, they would doubtless be killed instantly by the occupants; if the Russians opened first, the German crew would discharge their machine pistols.

Raeder shared his doubts to the men. "Should I ask Herr Hauptman what to do?" he stuttered.

The poor boy was his usual bag-of-nerves self, and clearly wished to abdicate the responsibility of the decision to someone of a higher rank. Kellerman struck the boy's arm with a thud, and told him to get a grip. However, even the warrior Kellerman had to concede that they were stuck for options. The electric adrenaline of combat had seemed to take a momentary lull, making the situation seem absurd to Otto; despite the fact that only a few millimetres of steel separate them from their opponents, they crew seemed to have begun to relax as if far from combat. Peter Scholl had reassumed his boyish smile, and Kellerman was even debating whether to spark up his pipe. This was simply a waiting game.

Eventually, Kellerman began to draw a grenade from his belt, without a word to the crew as to his intentions. Otto shook his head furiously, waving wildly with his arms to dissuade him from trying to blow up the Soviet inhabitants. Kellerman simply hushed Otto's protests, and held the grenade near the turret hatch. He did not, however, pull the pin or even unscrew the priming cap. This plan seemed rather strong; the Soviet occupants would panic at the arrival of the grenade, and jump from the tank if they had any sense. Otto nodded his approval, and readied himself for the kill.

Positioning himself behind the hatch, Kellerman prepared to drop the explosive into the turret. The crew ducked by the sides of the tank, in case a stream of enemy fire should feed from the trapdoor as it was opened. Kellerman inched open the door, and a crackling of pistol shots flew from the entrance, flying into the dark sky. He threw in the grenade, and closed the hatch. In half of a second, the murmurs inside the cabin once again grew to yells and shouts. Now all that remained was to see if the Russians would fall victim to the bait and leave their armoured citadel.

The crew did not have to wait long for a response. Immediately after the grenade landed to the floor of the tank with a metallic sound, the hatch was flung wide open with desperate strength. Kellerman, still sat behind the door, was pushed from the roof of the tank, squelching into the wet and muddy ground below. A Russian jumped from the door, firing a machine gun blindly into the darkness, forcing the crew to take cover and hug the hull of the machine. The soldier jumped to the floor, running past the crew and continuing to fire sporadically in the direction of the tank. It was vital that they shut down this shooting immediately, lest his sustained defence attract the attention of other Soviet scouting parties. The odd shot would simply blend with the continuous noise of battle in the distance, but continued bursts were certain to rouse suspicion.

By the time the man had got just over ten paces from the tank, a single rifle shot rang out from between the trees, and he fell to the floor in a heap. Greim's aim had been accurate as ever, and the soldier's machine gun grew silent once more. Another man emerged from the tank, likely a commander if his uniform was anything to go by. He had a pistol drawn, and prepared shoot Otto as he clambered from the turret. Raeder, however, was unusually quick to respond, and dropped the Russian with a quick clack-clack of his MP40. Blood spattered onto the back of the hatch door, and the man convulsed at the impact of each shot. He then, too, fell down without a yell, dropping back into the turret from whence he had come, and knocking over a series of shells on his way, which clanged around the tank. The BT-5 had only a crew of three, and the last member – the driver – had not yet emerged.

"Surrender!" shouted Otto.

It was a long shot to expect the inhabitant to understand the German being spoke to him, but Otto hoped that his tone might impart the meaning he wished to convey. There followed a moment of silence, as the crew awaited a response from within the tank. Finally, the driver's door began to cautiously swing open. The entire crew had trained their weapons on the opening, ready to annihilate the inhabitant with a hail of bullets should he try to resist. From the darkness of the tank, two outstretched and surrendering hands emerged, followed by a young man who was practically sobbing with fear. He was unarmed, it appeared, and Otto took the man by the collar, launching him to the ground and keeping the MP40 pressed into his chest.

The men breathed a much-needed sigh of relief. Kellerman was sent to search the body sniped by Greim, and hide the corpse from the main tracks. Scholl did the same for the commander who had fallen back into the turret, and Raeder began searching the tank for any information. Greim had come up to join the men now, praising Kellerman's quick-thinking grenade decoy, and the rest of the crew for acting so effectively. Otto, meanwhile, kept his sights fixed firmly on his Soviet prisoner. The poor lad was yet another young-faced conscript, flooded with fear and trepidation towards his captors. Greim approached the hostage, and spoke a few words of broken Russian; the commander could not speak the language well, but had acquired a few basics to use in situations such as this.

Raeder emerged from the hull of the BT-5, holding a piece of paper aloft, his face filled with glee at such a find.

"A map, Herr Hauptman!" he cried. "It's a map of the enemy base! It detailed the patrol route of the scouting tank!"

Greim thanked Raeder, taking the map and analysing it. While by no means detailed, it did appear to outline rough defensive positions, and lines of resistance. It also, crucially, detailed the exact position of the base, not three miles from the crew's current location. Greim showed the map to the prisoner, paired with more flawed Russian phrases, who nodded enthusiastically.

"The map is correct, I threatened that we would kill him if he lied. I reckon we can trust the boy," said Greim. He signalled Otto to release the hostage in the opposite direction of the enemy base, so as to prevent him reaching his comrades and raising the alarum siren. Otto pointed with his machine gun, and the Soviet mustered the German for 'thank you', and disappeared into the darkness as fast as he could.

"This map, it suggests that this tank refuels at the enemy base after completing its circuit. It was on its way back, it seems, heading for home. If we use this machine to approach the base, we should be able to pass the first sentry lines without arousing suspicion. Scholl and I can follow you in the Tiger, keeping it hidden until its needed, rather than bring it under the fire of anti-tank weapons at first instance," ordered Greim.

The commander could temporarily fill Otto's role as tank driver, while Otto, Kellerman and Raeder take the BT-5. The men now had to draft an attack plan, before the Reds realised that their tank was long missing. They would need a thorough plan, too; it was going to be a tough slog.

Chapter 6
67.1 Kilometres From Berlin

Before the crew could launch an assault on the Soviet command centre, there were a multitude of preparations to be made. First and foremost, the BT-5 would have to be restored to working order, in order to provide a covert entry into the vicinity of the base. The anti-tank grenade didn't seem to have damaged anything other than the tracks, and so Kellerman set about repairing the caterpillar belt. Raeder took to scrubbing the blood from the turret where they had gunned down the commander, by using water from the Russian knapsacks, lest a spotlight notice that the tank had seen combat since its last patrol.

Otto and Scholl, however, had a very different task to attend to. Greim called the pair over, his face buried in the documents recovered from the tank. "By my estimates, according to the size of the base on these maps, we will be facing at least fifty enemy soldiers. There are also symbols which seem to denote snipers, machine gun nests, and anti-tank weaponry. The bottom line is, these soldiers can repel an attack by five men."

Otto and Scholl were aware that their chances were slim.

"What can we do, Herr Hauptman?" asked Otto. "We don't stand a chance!"

Greim's expression was grave, yet not defeated. "We have

a distinct advantage, however. Most base patrol duty is assigned to second-rate, less battle-hardened units. It is possible, therefore, that the defenders will flee, if only we convince them that they face a tough fight. If we can find a way to appear like we are of a greater number than we are, they may surrender or rout." Otto and Scholl, therefore, had to create decoys to make it seem that the base was under heavier attack than it actually was.

It became clear, after a few experiments with tying string around the triggers of weapons, that such a method was more likely to kill the attackers than assist them. They needed to find a way to fire rounds and weapons without being present, thus giving the impression that there were multiple troops attacking the base. While unsure of how to launch the assault, the pair sat with Kellerman, who was currently resting and smoking his pipe. Greim called over to the group, telling Kellerman to be careful that his smouldering pipe did not spark the ammunition stores in the BT-5.

And then it hit them. Why not ignite the ammunition? If they split the ammunition into segments, light the sections and throw them across the base, they will be heard and seen as enormous sprays of gunfire. Otto informed Scholl of his idea, and they set about their work. Tearing up the Russians' tunics and coats, they dipped the resultant rags in the fuel of the tank and wrapped them around collections of ammunition from the enemy tank. These segments of machine gun chain, only around ten rounds each, would fire as they became engulfed in flames. Each section had a loose rag attached to the main wrapping, which would act as a short fuse to prevent the bullets firing too early and killing the thrower.

They made up as many as time would allow, around

twenty all in all. They also wrapped a small number of the BT-5's main gun shells, to add the illusion of armoured support. Raeder stashed the eclectic collection in a large sack and stowed it in the turret of the Russian tank. Kellerman and Raeder prepared to mount the captured machine which would serve as a trojan horse. Greim and Scholl had set off to bring the Tiger once more, after briefing Otto as to the route he had to take to the enemy base. They would drive the Tiger into view as a final coup de grace when the majority of defenders had been scared away, with the roar of its cannon mopping up any resistance, though only when most anti-tank defences had been cleared.

Finally, it was time to move. Otto brought the BT-5 engine to life, feeling the under-seat rumble as he revved the engine. The interior was far less comfortable that his own Tiger cabin, though this may have simply been due to unfamiliarity. While much smaller than the crew's Panzer VI, the Russian tank did feel nippier, and was certainly far less heavy. Compared with his usual powerful German machine, Otto felt as if he was driving a small car. He engaged the throttle, and felt the hulk lurch forward.

The small tank zoomed across the forest road, cutting through the soft mud as it accelerated. The crew felt positively nauseous with nerves at the thought of the impending assault, readying their weapons and making their respective peace. It was painfully clear to each man that their survival in this attack was far from certain. Raeder was his usual bag of nerves, with Kellerman trying desperately to steel the young man and steady his resolve. According to Greim's brief to Otto, the party should be approaching the enemy base in the next few minutes; Otto was having to carry the tank forward as quickly as its engine would allow, in order to reduce the disparity between its return and usual patrol times. It was vital to minimise the amount of time lost due to the hijacking, in order to not arouse suspicion of the tank having been long missing.

In moments such as this, many of the crew were plagued with the memories of the men they had killed, and Otto was no exception. What stuck with him particularly vividly was the face of young Alexei, his letter still burning a hole in Otto's pocket. The soldier had seemed so unafraid of death, with only a mild apprehension colouring his expression. He had been so full of hate when he had attacked Raeder and Otto the night before, and yet the second day he was calm. What was particularly chilling, perhaps, is that because the man had not been twisted in fear, he seemed all the more human. The majority of soldiers facing immediate death, such as the Russian tank driver shot by the SS officer in the clearing, were contorted in terror, reduced to jittering wrecks which were little distinguishable from animals. But Alexei, he had maintained the majority of his composure, and this is what so disturbed Otto; he was just like Alexei. Death was, in this case, not portrayed with the animalistic fear of a wounded creature, but on the face of an individual who completely maintained the appearance of a man.

But as they approached the base, Otto's usual mantra raised its head. "Don't think about it," he told himself. Anyone would turn insane at the mere sight of such horrors, let alone before participating in an attack such as theirs. The base could be seen now, a small command post in between the trees. It sat on a hillside, with the trees cut like a horseshoe as the position extended up the mount. There were a series of trenches carved between the citadel and the sparser forest from which the crew approach, with the rest of the base surrounded by much thicker woods on the other three sides. There were two guard towers visible, sitting at the top of the hill, with sentries and spotlights stationed there. Several machine gun positions dotted the landscape, covering each trench in turn, with a small number of soldiers milling between the various defences. Greim's prediction had been correct; around fifty soldiers littered the post, most of them smoking or drinking and laughing with their comrades, certainly unexpectant of an attack.

Raeder prepared to jump from the tank first, when free from spotlights. The tank had been sighted now, a spotlight briefly investigating the machine before turning away. Most of the Soviets seemed barely to notice its approach, so accustomed were they to the coming and going of their faithful scout. Otto was making for a refuelling station, at the base of the hill and outskirt of the base. He signalled the breaks in the prying lights, with Raeder dismounting quickly and silently, burying himself in the mud just short of the first trench. Kellerman was set to follow, but gave Otto one last idea.

"Take this," he whispered, passing Otto another anti-tank bundle. "When you get to the refuelling spot, set it off near the ammo rack. It'll go up like a second sun! That'll make them think they're for it!" After passing the device to Otto, Kellerman dismounted similarly quietly and moved to Raeder's position.

It was now down to Otto. The Reds still had not the faintest inkling that an attack was underway, and Raeder and Kellerman remained well hidden. Applying the brakes as he approached the station, the tank ground to a halt. A young Russian soldier was there waiting, and began refuelling the vehicle from the rear. How would Otto get out without being spotted? Raeder and Kellerman lie not fifteen metres away, pressed to the dirt. Surely the Soviet pump attendant would notice Otto as he dismounted? He had only one choice; brave it out, and hope a combination of the dark and his confident movement would give the Russian no cause to check his identity. His heart was beating in his ears, as he opened the hatch and arose from the Russian tank. He had the anti-tank grenade ready, which he would pull the pin from as he jumped from the machine.

As he prepared to climb down from the machine, the pump attendant said something to Otto in Russian, with what sounded like a jovial tone. Not having the faintest clue what he had been told or asked, Otto drew on the only Russian word he knew.

"Da," he said, laughing in an attempt to match the man's own demeanour. It had seemed to suffice; the man simply smiled to himself and continued to refuel the tank. Otto pulled the pin of the grenade bundle, and proceeded to walk away from the tank towards Kellerman and Raeder as quickly as he could casually appear to do so.

Five. Otto passed the refueller, who did not look up from his task. Four. he was steadily closing the distance to Raeder and Kellerman, praying that a spotlight did not spy his movements. Three. The pump attendant seemed to be wandering where the rest of the tank crew were, and indeed why only the driver had left the machine. Two. The attendant turned and began shouting in alarm at Otto, who broke into a sprint himself, and dived to the floor beside Kellerman and Raeder, desperately covering himself as best he could to prepare for the explosion. One.

A tremendous boom tore through the air, seeming to

temporarily deafen the crew with its ferocity. A fantastic golden glow burst from the tank, washing Otto in searing hot air, and showering the crew in flecks of hot oil, thankfully insufficient in size to cause real injury. Fire was bursting violently from the hatches, roaring several metres into the sky as it was heated so wondrously. Smaller explosions could be heard from inside the tank itself, as shells began to detonate inside the cabin, combining with the heat of the burning fuel to create a deadly maelstrom. The crew were crawling frantically from the fiery wreck, finding sturdier cover to defend them from the cracks of pure flame. Some shells stowed upright had fired through the roof of the tank, flying high into the air before thudding to the forest floor in the near distance. Others were punching through the side of the tank in all directions, some flying narrowly above the heads of the crawling German crew, and some soaring to explode deep within the base. The entire post was on high alert now, though the pump attendant had been eviscerated immediately, engulfed in the molten metallic mess.

A final gargantuan explosion sounded, quite distinguishable from the previous barrage due to its thunderous crack, and as Otto looked into the sky from his prone position, he spied the turret of the BT-5 rocket into the air in a trail of flame and smoke, blown from the tank as the fire had ignited the main store of fuel at the station. Peering over the tiny ridge which had sheltered him, Otto could hardly recognise what lay before him as a tank; lying on its side, the turretless BT-5 had been shredded in half, with the hull bursting outwards from the force of the explosion.

There remained no time to marvel at the feat of destruction which had just been engineered. The crew had to capitalise on this mass confusion and fear, with a surprisingly calm Raeder distributing the distraction bullet bags to Otto and Kellerman. The pair began lighting the clumps of ammunition and oil-soaked rags, hurling them in any and all directions across the base. Within seconds, the previously sleepy base had been turned into a warzone. The bullet sections were firing across the area, so convincingly that even Otto had to double take and check that there were not in fact more attackers than simply the three crewmen. The Russians were in full disarray, firing wildly into the darkness with all their might. Spotlights frantically danced across the trenches and trees, desperately searching for an assailant to return fire upon. The crew had to remain close to the ground, as a menagerie of bullets, both from Russian defenders and the distraction devices, zipped across their heads at all vectors. The occasional unlucky defender was hit by a stray round, or gunned down by his own side in the confusion, but generally the display simply served to suppress and confuse any organised resistance.

 The three men finally fell into the first defensive trench line, on the left flank of the base. Kellerman, who had taken the stash of devices from Raeder, continued sporadically launching the distraction bursts across the base to maintain the confusion, as Otto and Raeder led the way through the maze of trenches towards the command station. It was imperative that they secure the main building before the Soviets could destroy any radios and equipment in their retreat. Snaking through the muddy labyrinth, the crew walked past most Russians who had not sighted them, but were busy flinging rounds into the darkness in some attempt to defend themselves. Occasionally a small MP40 burst was employed by the pair to fell a particularly alert soldier, but generally such direct attack was unnecessary.

After some careful manoeuvring, the crew reached the final defensive trench before the main headquarters. This section was better lit than the foremost defences, and some officers had exited the command room to attempt to coordinate some sort of organised resistance in this line. The three Tiger operators simply needed to draw the bulk of these more steeled men from the defence if they hoped to get anywhere near the radio station. Raeder, however, had a plan. He signalled Kellerman to concentrate a number of the distraction grenades on the opposite flank of the base, in order to briefly draw the attention of these more capable defenders. He then drew from the sack containing such distractors one of the two tank shells which they had liberated, wrapped in oiled cloth in a similar fashion to the bullet belt sections.

Pulling Otto by the collar, Raeder darted across the width of the trench and out onto the other side, using the brief second of misdirection which had been created. The defenders were firing at the right flank of the base, in the direction of the gunfire bursts as created by the crew's devices. This allowed Raeder and Otto to slip past the men, to the shadowed area directly under the leftmost of the two watchtowers.

"Dig!" yelled Raeder, clawing through the soft mud under the tower with his bare hands.

Otto followed suit, with no small degree of confusion, to help Raeder create a hole roughly a foot deep and half as wide. The young radio operators next action, however, made clear to Otto exactly what was planned, and Otto could not but marvel at his brilliance of wit. Raeder buried the tank shell in the earth, face up, and lit the makeshift cloth-fuel fuse.

The men retreated as quick as their legs would carry them

to Kellerman's position, and informed the loader that he should keep his head down. Then, the shell fired. It had only sufficient room for oxygen to feed the flames of its fabric covering, and so had been unable to change aiming position; the shot flew with awesome speed directly upwards, and ripped through the above watchtower. A cloud of dust and smoke ensued, as the wooden guard post was disintegrated with the force of the projectile. The shell had been an armour piercing round, due to the danger of a high explosive shell simply blowing up before firing, and it had completely disassembled the structure above it. Splinters and wooden planks showered the base, accompanied by a choking amount of sawdust. Sparks were sprinkled as the spotlight mounted on the tower was destroyed, lighting up the entire base for the briefest moment.

It was at this point that many of the Russians' confusion transformed into a full rout. The destruction of both the BT-5 and the tower had hinted that the attackers had armour support, and the volume of incoming gunfire from the lit rounds was monumental. The Russians in the front few trenches ran across the top of the defensive works, weapons discarded, towards the rear of the base, which was the only direction from which no gunfire emanated. Some hardened officers had tried to shoot deserters at first, until the sheer number of men dispersing into the rear woods was too many for their pistols to keep up with, and the officers began to join the retreat. Only a handful of strong-willed Russians, little more than ten in total, continued to man their positions against the imagined attacker.

The final trench was now more or less clear, and the crew prepared to storm the command building. The door was, as expected, securely locked. Otto and Raeder prepared the second tank shell in a similar fashion to that used on the tower, hoping to knock through the metal door. The accuracy of this second attack was far less than certain; due to the sideways angle, it was impossible to guarantee that the shell would fly straight when the recoil affected its dirt mountings. Nevertheless, Otto and Raeder set the round to fire at the base of the door, in the hope that a small amount of upwards recoil would still allow the projectile to strike the small concrete building. Kellerman was still busy deploying the last of the ammunition sections around the base, in order to maintain confusion as long as was possible. They lit the covering and retired to a sheltered dugout in the side of the trench.

The round did not fire in quite the desired fashion, but it did provide some success. The powerful recoil had caused the round to fly at a slightly high and righthand angle, but the round had still clipped the bunker enough to cause the top edge and roof to cave in somewhat. After the boom and accompanying crumble of debris had settled, the pair dashed to the walls of their target once more. The opening was around two metres from the ground, and reachable with a boost. Raeder first flung a spare stick grenade into the breach, causing the coughs and shouts of inhabitants through the dust to fall silent after the dulled bang. Otto then boosted him over the wall, where Raeder clung to the ruin and pulled Otto with him into the building.

It was dimly lit and filled with dust. Three soldiers lay dead, peppered with grenade shrapnel and mangled by the blast. Judging by the size of the building, this was one of only two rooms, with a similar metal door separating them. Yet more muffled shouts emanated from the second room, as the men inside struggled to work out what had happened next door. Otto and Raeder stacked up on the door, ready to breach and eliminate all who dwell inside. It was always a risky operation, entering a guarded room, for fear that the enemy already had guns trained on the door ready to mow down attackers before they could react. Otto and Raeder were in particular danger, as the need to preserve the radio equipment in the next room negated the possibility of employing a grenade.

As it transpired, however, the crew would be robbed of the first move. Before they had breached the door, a Soviet soldier came from inside, investigating the commotion in the first room. The pair had to act so fast that they almost didn't have time to compute their own actions before they executed them. Otto pressed his MP40 into the abdomen of the Russian, his other hand on the man's shoulder, and began firing without pause. The soldier had not been able to block the sudden attack, and simply began spitting his own blood at Otto as he was pumped with a hail of lead. Otto's hands, too, had become covered in a warm and slippery crimson sludge, as the bullets continued to tear into the man's belly, passing through his back and killing many of the occupants on the other side. Otto continued to press forward, using the man, who was swiftly turning into a shredded corpse, as a makeshift human shield. The rounds of his machine pistol were cutting into the bewildered guards, who had scarcely gathered their wits enough to resist. Raeder followed Otto immediately, unleashing his own torrent of rounds into the small chamber.

The two men fired until their weapons clicked, devoid of ammunition, and soon realised that for the last few seconds they had been hosing corpses with bullets, so comprehensively had their opening bursts cleared the room. The walls were painted with blood, each man having been hit several times, their innards spurting across the small concrete box. It was a truly gruesome sight. Raeder rushed to the radio, careful not to slip on the pools of gore which flooded the floor, while Otto exited the bunker through the now unlocked door to check on the scenario outside.

Kellerman had begun shooting at the defenders himself, of which around half a dozen remained. Otto joined the firefight, though it seemed that it would be over soon; a distant rumble heralded the arrival of their much-loved Tiger, which was rolling towards the base. The beast let out a mighty roar of its cannon, and with that, the remaining Soviet defenders ran from the command post. Their silhouettes could be made out against the dawn, which was beginning to crack through the trees, as they darted into the cover of the forest. There was little point wasting ammunition on these stragglers, for they would soon disappear.

And finally, the base lay clear. Several bodies littered the various trenches, with many an explosion scorch and bullet mark from the various distractions orchestrated by the crew. The pitiful remains of the BT-5 continued to burn, smouldering steadily along with the remnants of the refuelling station, which was largely taken up by a large crater. Calm was beginning to return to the war-torn forest, with the birds' morning chirps replacing the bangs and cries of combat which had been so loud moments ago.

Otto sat near the first trench, his legs overcome with a terrible weakness all of a sudden, as the adrenaline left his body. He could not quite believe his eyes; had they truly done it? They had cleared this entire position, without so much as their faithful Tiger to defend them? It was quite something to behold, let alone the fact that the crew had completed it without incident. Otto removed his cap and wiped his brow with relief at having survived the ordeal. Had he the energy, he might have cried in happiness; for now, however, he settled with sitting, taking a brief moment of relaxation, and awaiting the arrival of Greim and Scholl from the now dismounted Tiger.

Chapter 7
52.7 Kilometres From Berlin

"Well done, lads," congratulated Greim, stepping across the desolate and body strewn trenches, with Scholl at his side.

He was not wrong to give such praise; the crew had indeed performed brilliantly in overcoming the command post. Otto was sat on the walls of the last trench, still able to hear Raeder fiddling with the radio in the bunker. The occasional crack ricocheted between the forest trees, as the odd late piece of ammunition ignited, and small explosions continued to arise from the disintegrated fuel depot at the base of the hill. The entire outpost was not half of a kilometre in depth, and yet the clearing of its defenders had seemed to take hours of constant action.

The beginnings of dawn were breaking the darkness of the night, allowing just enough light for the crew to fully see the situation which surrounded them. The air was thick with smoke, and the stench of death wafted particularly strongly from the bunker. Otto could barely stomach the thought of re-entering the room of gore which he had created, and so felt it was best to simply wait until Raeder emerged with news of radio contact. There was no moaning to be heard, no defenders which lay still dying; indeed, the majority of the soldiers had simply fled the area, and so while the trenches did contain a few cadavers, the number of dead in no way equated to the original number garrisoned at the base.

The exhausted Kellerman had, predictably, lit his pipe.

"That'll kill you, you know," said Otto.

He had never been convinced of the purported benefits of smoking, feeling that it blocked the individual from the freshness of the air, one of the few reminders of natural beauty in this world of war. Kellerman seemed to laugh at the notion.

"We just took an entire Soviet base, alone. You're telling me this will kill me quicker than a Russian bullet?" he chuckled, gesturing to the embers from which he drew breaths.

Otto simply smiled and began trying to find a source of water. In all the excitement, he had not realised quite how dry his throat had become, especially with all the fire and fumes surrounding the crew.

"We saw that tank go up from the other side of the forest! I bet that got their attention!" exclaimed Scholl, rushing towards Otto, desperate to hear the details of how the operation had gone. The light-spirited gunner would doubtless have loved to join the men on their perilous undertaking but was required to operate the Tiger's cannon; while Greim may have trained in all crew positions, this did not mean he could do them all simultaneously. Otto filled Scholl in with the events, who hung onto his every word.

Otto noticed, when speaking to Scholl, quite how tired the poor man looked, and it was certain that Otto appeared the same. The colour of his eyes was washed out and pale, and they were surrounded by even darker bags than when Otto had caught his own reflection in the bathroom at Herr Sichter's. His face was equally devoid of colour, and his stare portrayed a slight lack of focus, a sadness at the need to carry on so relentlessly. His thoughts were soon interrupted by yells from within the bunker, as Raeder reported successful radio contact.

"I've got through! I reached the Berlin defence!" he cheered, practically dancing out of the bunker door with delight.

"Well done, Raeder," commended Greim. "What did they say? Can they arrange a breakout?" he asked.

Raeder nodded excitedly, explaining that they could manage a local counterattack just after noon that day. The Reds had, it seemed, been unable to fully close the iron ring around the city just yet, and a select few routes for refugees, supplies and reinforcements remained open. To reach the city by midday was more than within the crew's capacity, for there lay only one further town between them and the capital. If they were late, however, the defensive line would withdraw within the buildings of Berlin itself, transforming the historic settlement into a true front city, and precluding any break in.

With that, Greim ordered a brief scavenging of any ammunition or supplies which would aid the city defence, before the crew remounted their trusty battle wagon. Otto would take the remaining guard tower, whilst the others scoured the trench network. His boots tapped metallically on the ladder as he hoisted himself up the rickety structure. Reaching the peak, he stepped into the cabin of the watchtower with a thud. The tower consisted mostly of thin wood, with only select metal components; this helped to explain the utter destruction unleashed upon the first watchtower when struck by the crew's tank shell device.

The platform on which Otto now stood was a sorry sight. The guard appeared to have shot himself, so shaken was he by the assault that he perhaps didn't fancy his chances of avoiding a slow death at the hands of the attackers. The poor soldier's blood was strewn across the decking of the viewpoint, with a pistol lying in his open hand. But this pitiful sight was totally overshadowed by the tremendous view which Otto was presented with from the elevated guard tower.

The command outpost, beginning to become visible in the fledgling dawn, was littered with destruction. Wooden plants and splinters had been showered across the innermost trenches, with what rump of the destroyed watchtower remained laying smouldering in the dirt. The BT-5 turret had been hurtled to the opposite flank of the fuelling station, blackened and broken at the force of the explosion. A seemingly solid stack of black smoke continued to rise, levitating steadily upwards from the main hull of the Russian tank and pump station. The city was clearly visible, the searchlights still illuminating the soot cloud which hung ominously over the distant buildings. Otto could also just about spot the town through which the crew must venture and see the Russian troops surrounding the area from other vectors. Time was short.

Otto gathered the submachine gun and grenade which sat next to the fallen guard and began to descend the thin metal ladder of the tower. Reaching the floor, he began to cross towards the Tiger, stopping occasionally to catch a glance at the contents of the various trenches. Greim was calling the crew to muster at their machine and remount the tank to begin movement. His feet clunking on the thick metal armour, notably slippery owing to the mud which caked his boots and lower trousers, Otto hauled himself aboard the mighty tank, and dropped into his driver's seat. It was less than a minute before the entire team had reassumed their stations, and Greim gave the order to continue their journey.

As he had done countless times, Otto began to feed the Tiger revs, feeling the engine purr as it awoke. The huge, armoured machine rolled onward, turning steadily and gaining speed. After some acceleration, the tank was running in the direction of the destroyed town. The roads were shell-marked in places, much of the concrete having been torn up and spread across the area. It occurred to Otto that some retreating columns had passed this way, as denoted by the occasional wrecked panzer, mangled dead horse, and soldier's corpse splayed across the street.

The buildings lining the road as the crew entered the town were wrecks. Hollowed out shacks, totally devoid of any character which they might have once embodied. Otto could almost see the bunting which would have decorated the streets of what had been this charming town in former days, the bustling crowds and parades which might once have processed down the street for Easter around this time. These lanes would have echoed with the conversations of friends, businessmen and lovers. And yet the town was a ruined ghost. It had not been subjected to the horrors of actual urban warfare, due to the Russians failing to close this section of the line as yet, but had been mauled by artillery fire and air strikes inflicted upon retreating German forces.

Barely any of the windows still held intact panes, most having been smashed by the rounds crashing down from enemy howitzers. It reminded Otto greatly of the scenes which greeted him as he advanced into Minsk, years previously. He had managed to avoid service in or around Stalingrad, having been reassigned to Army Group North, but he had heard reports of the devastation which had occurred; Otto was not alone in fearing the same fate befalling their beloved Berlin.

The 'Rattenkrieg' which had coloured such fighting, the tremendous losses and underhanded combat suffered by both sides, was dangerously close to the heart of the Reich. The crew had spent so much of the early war as an aggressor, able to inflict but rarely suffer such devastation as they stormed through enemy land. And now, they were being forced to reap what they had so enthusiastically sown.

As they ventured further into the desolate cluster of buildings, the destruction appeared ever more condensed. Yet more structures had been reduced to simple rubble, spilling onto the streets and requiring Otto to employ some creative driving to circumvent them. The odd fire still raged from the shells of the emptied buildings, and the air was thick with smoke. Otto opened his hatch, relatively confident that the town was clear of Russian snipers, in an attempt to better survey the scene. The smell of fire intermingled with the reek from the piles of dead mules and men, lost from the retreating troops under the hail of fire. The pinnacle of engineering represented by the Tiger, Otto believed, was always fiercely juxtaposed by the mainly horse-drawn backbone of the Wehrmacht. This was another reason that the crew so hated their SS counterparts; the bastards were always prioritised when it came to mechanisation.

Doors lay ajar, with luggage covering the ground, dropped in the hasty evacuation. Otto could only imagine the face of urban exodus; having usually been posted to the front, he had not often seen the panicked fleeing of an entire town or city's populace. His own experience extended only to military withdrawals, which had always seemed comparatively organised to him when he considered the ever-greater precariousness which coloured the Reich's military situation.

The terrified faces, hurried half-preparations, and sickening uncertainty of civilian forced migration were all beyond the young Tiger driver.

The tank continued to rumble forward along the war-stricken streets, the sound of the tracks echoing through the silence, rebounding across the hollow concrete forest. The buildings of the town seemed endless when viewed from the driver's viewpoint, an unending row of desolation. They had not yet neared the town centre, due to the particularly careful driving practiced by Otto in order to navigate the rubble labyrinth. Before long, however, when the crew had only ventured around half an hour into the town, the still dust of the air was permeated by a near distant sound.

A woman's scream could just about be heard through the crew's open hatches, no more than a few hundred metres ahead of the tank. Closing on the origin of the sound, the men sighted a small group of civilian refugees, near a structure engulfed by one of the still-raging fires which choked the town. Otto brought the Tiger to a halt, emerging from the cabin to get a better view of the situation; an elderly man lay on the ground, surrounded by blood but surviving. He was being tended by an old woman, while a younger lady continued to cry desperately at the orange flames. The entire house had not yet been consumed by the fire, but the entrance appeared quite impassable, and the rear of the building would likely be alight within a few minutes.

Without a word or order, the crew simultaneously dismounted the Panzer and hurried to the small group. Otto had put the engine to slumber, and awaited Greim's instruction on how they could best help the civilians.

"My child! She is in there!" cried the hysterical woman,

her face etched with the raw emotion which Otto was only accustomed to seeing Raeder displaying. "The fires spread so quickly, and Papa fell. My baby is in there!" she continued to yell.

The poor girl was so terribly stricken with utter helplessness, facing the prospect of her young child burning with their family home. The old man seemed to have fallen on some glass shards and was bleeding quite profusely from a series of small cuts on his hands and face.

Greim gestured Otto and Kellerman towards the man, while he himself embraced the woman in a desperate but useless attempt to console her from the dreadful event unfolding before her. Otto came to the man and began to pick some of the more noticeable glass shards from his face, while Kellerman held his hand and comforted the gentleman against the pain he was enduring. Scholl was preparing the crew's measly first aid kit, taking bandages and water to the pair. Their attention was soon diverted, however, as they heard the splashing of an emptied water bottle behind them.

Raeder was standing by the tank, empty canteen in hand, his entire uniform and face drenched in its contents. Before Otto had time to question such a bizarre action, however, the soaked boy was darting as fast as his legs would carry him in the direction of the flaming building, his eyes fixed on the fires blocking the entrance. Greim tried to grab Raeder as he sprinted past him, but the radio operator was exceptionally nimble on account of his age and smallish stature and avoided the tall commander. He continued to run as the crew begged him to stop and flung himself through the fires at the door's entrance, into the black smoke and fire of the building.

Otto could not believe his eyes. Had their youngest recruit

simply committed suicide, so exhausted at the strains of conflict which surrounded him? Or had this, and the bottle emptying, been part of some sort of nervous breakdown, a stress induced psychotic episode, culminating tragically in the death of their anxious friend? The woman had ceased her cries, so struck was she at the mysteriousness of Raeder's leap into the hell which surrounded her home. Even the cocksure Kellerman, often so critical at the shortcomings of the young boy, seemed almost moved to tears at the prospect of Raeder having passed in such a fashion. There followed a few eternal seconds of silence, with no one exactly sure what to do next. The fire continued to crackle furiously, and sections of the ceiling began to fall into the building with explosions of sparks and heat.

Suddenly, the flames at the entrance were again broken by a darkened figure diving through the breach. Raeder had lunged back out of the house, coughing and spluttering as he struggled to rid his lungs of smoke. His face was blackened by soot streaks, and his arms reddened in places by burns. His uniform, too, was coated with soot and smoke, discoloured by the fire and the soaking until it was almost black. The boy's blue eyes remained open, and though he stumbled with the lack of oxygen, he managed to maintain his footing. Otto could see Greim and Kellerman prepare to reprimand the boy into next week with a synchronised intake of breath, until they saw a sooty-white bundle in the arms of the young radio operator.

Raeder's was not the only cough to be heard. There sounded another, much higher pitched and quieter, emerging from the ball of towels in Raeder's arms. He removed the top layer to reveal the face of a baby. The child was red with strain as it tried to breathe, coughing and gasping for air, but very much alive. Raeder was smiling exhaustedly at his success, and passed the fragile being to the woman, who had resumed an understandable flood of tears, but in happiness. She held the young one close and patted its back to ease its breathing. The old man, woman, and crew were all stunned into silence, staring at Raeder and the surviving infant in turn.

The family of refugees dashed towards the rescued baby, fussing over the child and rejoicing at her survival. Kellerman and Greim were busy praising Raeder, while Scholl and Otto still felt unable to move.

"Well done lad, but why? And, how?" asked Kellerman, unsure as to Raeder's apparent fireproof nature. The radio operator, displaying a wide grin of white teeth harshly contrasted against his sooty face, simply held his emptied bottle in response.

"Of course!" yelled Scholl, rising from the pile of bandages. "The water! It stopped his uniform from catching fire!"

Otto had to commend the quick thinking of Raeder, which had proved useful in the past few days. Both at the Soviet command post, and in rescuing the child, he had displayed a sharpness of thought far different to his usual nervous wreck of a self. The water would have provided a thin yet important layer to prevent his skin burning instantly as he jumped through the initial fires, allowing his survival in the mission.

"So, Hans, how did the child not die? That smoke nearly killed you off, by God!" asked Otto, palpable admiration in his tone.

Raeder replied, "Thankfully, the poor thing was on the floor. The smoke was near the ceiling, so she had at least a minute or so until the fire spread. I just grabbed a towel, dipped it in some water on the side, and wrapped the little one up."

Kellerman came to join the group, patting Raeder's shoulder. He then made a gesture which Otto had never witnessed in the three years the crew had served together; he offered Raeder his pipe, loaded with his special reserve of tobacco which his family had sent him. Isaac Kellerman only used his small supply of this type when he had truly believed he would die, and avoided it. To offer this to Raeder was more than an honour. Raeder accepted the gift with more coughs than when he emerged the flaming building but had never been more privileged than to achieve such praise from his harshest critic in Kellerman.

The woman rushed to the gathered crew, and kissed Raeder passionately; the young crewman's blush could even be seen through the thick soot which coated his skin. Otto returned to the old man, who still had several shards of glass embedded in his hands.

"Your comrade there, he is a good man," observed the man, gesturing to Raeder.

Otto nodded, responding, "He is indeed. I often think too good to be out here. He doesn't belong in this war; it isn't designed for good men."

The old man shrugged, as if he had heard the argument before. "We all thought the same thing in the last war, you know. It seemed a hell on earth. But even a world of thorns contains the odd rose. My commanding officer, he was good. Killed in the Ludendorff offensive, defending the wounded. A good man." The old man seemed almost to tail off, still reliving the memory of his late commander, away from the here and now.

"Say, Raeder," shouted Scholl, who had returned to the

Tiger for more first aid supplies. "How did you get in and out so quick? I've never seen you do that sort of dash?"

Raeder chuckled, informing the crew, "Back home, in Munich, I was a keen sprinter. Used to race for Bavaria, in fact, in the youth team. I suppose it never left me, you just never see it because the Tiger ferries us about!" he chortled. "It was never what I wanted to do for a career though," he sighed. Scholl's face turned inquisitive, having never really delved into Raeder's hopes and aspirations on account of his comparative newness to the crew.

"What did you want for a job then?" asked Scholl.

Raeder's grin grew in size, as he bore a smile and replied to the group, "I wanted to be a fireman." Even the stoic Greim bellowed with laughter at the response.

The odd boom of artillery could be heard in the distance, as the fires continued to rage metres from the crew. After they had treated the worst of the elderly gentleman's injuries and moved the group of survivors a safe distance from the fiery shell of a home, the crew bid their farewells and remounted the tank. It must have been at least eight or nine o'clock, thought Otto; it was imperative that the crew kept moving, lest they squander their thin window of opportunity to slip past the closing Soviet ring. Greim conversed some more with the old man, asking the quickest way through the town, and discovered that there was only around ten miles between them and the city outskirts.

"You should come with us, get to Berlin before the Russians secure this settlement. You need to be behind the defence line," advised Greim to the refugees.

The old man simply rolled his eyes, gave a defeated sigh, and said, "For what? Delay the inevitable? The same fate will befall all of us. The Russians are coming. It's an unstoppable tide, a wave of iron, steel, and anger. We poked the Soviet bear, hell we nearly destroyed it! Now it's our turn. And so, my family and I will stay here, thank you. If I have to die, I'll die on my own terms."

Otto felt a shudder traverse the length of his spine at such a bleak assessment of the fate facing their proud nation, and its people. He had rarely heard such observations through the war, not least due to the prospect of being accused as a 'defeatist'. It seemed only now the SS infrastructure was crumbling that people were willing to see the state of affairs as it was. But what chilled Otto most intensely, was that he, and the whole crew, knew that the old man was absolutely correct.

Don't think about it, he told himself yet again. This motto, exercised countless times, seemed the only way to carry on. He simply got his head down, powered up the Tiger, and started the machine's stalking the street once more. The refugees were soon out of sight, only marked by the smokestack billowing from the flaming building. The crew passed several other destroyed houses, and the odd wrecked Panzer knocked out in the retreat. Soon, however, the scenery began to change, with the road showing an opening into a town square.

"Herr Hauptman, we will be exposed in that plaza," called Otto. "Should we dismount and scout for any anti-tank equipment?" Greim stroked his chin, deep in thought as he calculated how much risk should warrant the crew wasting any precious time on matters such as scouting.

After a moment, he took a sigh, muttering, "Yes, I suppose that's a good idea. Griff, Scholl, dismount the Panzer and carefully check what's up there, would you?" The pair opened their respective hatches, and arose from the crew cabin, ready to survey the route ahead.

Otto heard the hollow crunch of loose gravels and rubble under his foot, as he clutched his MP40 and, alongside Scholl, stalked towards the town square. The air seemed oddly quiet away from the monotonous droning of the Tiger's engine, only punctured by crackling fires, distant explosions and booms, and the pair's own footsteps. It struck Otto as intensely eerie, that the once vibrant and lively streets were now so dead, only home to potential danger. The men were keenly scanning the buildings as they approached the plaza; they had long come to fear the sights of Soviet snipers, embedded amongst the ruins.

When the road opened out into the square, Otto took cover with Scholl behind a fallen pillar detached from what seemed to be the town hall. The Hellenic building overshadowed the area, likely once a prominent symbol of the town's pride. Scholl fumbled in his knapsack for a moment, and drew a pair of binoculars.

"Seems pretty clear," he said, searching the buildings. "No field pieces, no soldiers, tanks, seems to be… oh hang on." He withdrew the binoculars with a sigh, and handed them to Otto, pointing at one of the far edges of the square. Following his gesture, Otto spotted a small group of Soviet soldiers, no more than three, searching crates, unaware of the Tiger or her crew.

"They haven't noticed us, have they?" asked Otto, wary of alerting the Russians when so close to their front lines. Scholl shook his head, yet sighed in such a way that Otto knew he was worried also.

"They might not have seen us yet, but they definitely will when we storm through the square in our tank!" he snapped, his usual cool and jovial nature evidently compromised by the stress of the situation in which the crew now found themselves. With that, the pair trudged towards the parked Tiger, preparing to deliver the bad news to their commander.

Chapter 8
34.9 Kilometres From Berlin

Greim could tell by the expression worn by the pair that their news would be less than joyous. Otto chose to make the delivery, reporting loudly.

"Russians, Herr Hauptman. Only a handful, but they're sure to have a problem with a heavily armed Tiger passing through." Furrowing his brow, Greim turned his attention to his pocket watch; a detour around the town centre could add as much as two hours to their journey time, especially if they ran into rubble blockades or enemies. They were all acutely aware that the defence around Berlin would soon collapse, and the crew would need to be in the city when it did, if only to delay the uncertainty of not having any orders to follow. Perhaps it was for want of food rations, perhaps it was for want of purpose, and perhaps it was for no reason at all, but the fact remained that the crew wanted to be in Berlin – and their window was closing.

Eventually, Greim made the only decision available. A detour was far too great a risk to their delicate timeframe and would surely result in their being locked out of Berlin.

"We need to go through," he sighed. "Hopefully a few well-placed machine gun bursts will frighten off the soldiers, and we can move through before they have a chance to bring up support."

And with that, Otto took his seat, and prepared to launch their trusty war-wagon through the town square. If they could suppress, or perhaps even hit some of the Soviets, they should be able to pass through unscathed.

The Panzer lurched forward, carrying her crew with her. They were approaching the square from the far end, with relation to the town hall. The Russians were at the opposite corner, and so should be within the bow gunner's arc of fire for most of the journey across the plaza. Raeder, still riding his newfound confidence following the fire rescue, looked focused, ready to pin down the hostiles as soon as they noticed the Tiger. It was vital that he held his nerve and only opened fire when noticed by the Russians had seen them, in order to provide as many vital seconds of being undetected as possible.

As they passed the walls and opened into the square, Otto could barely draw breaths, so strained was his torso with the stress of their being sighted. For now, they had not been spied by the enemy soldiers, and the Russians continued searching crates. Raeder was still prepared, Kellerman stood ready with a new shell, Scholl prepared to traverse the turret, and Greim kept a careful watch for new developments. And Otto, he simply kept moving onwards, doing all he could to stay focussed on the task at hand, rather than worrying about his and the entire crew's possible impending death.

As if in slow motion, Otto spied one of the Russians begin shouting, and the group dispersed behind the town hall. Without a word, the crew sprang into action; Otto pulled as hard as he could on the righthand brake, turning the Tiger just enough to give Raeder an easier shot of the squad, and Scholl less distance to traverse the turret. The MG34 began spitting tracer rounds across the square, the deafening rattle echoing around the crew cabin. Scholl elected to hold his fire, rather than dig further into the Tiger's precious and depleted shell supply for the sake of such minor targets. While Raeder did not manage to hit the Russians between the rubble, they had run away and ceased to threaten the tank. They flocked behind the pillars of the town hall and rushed towards some green metallic structure which Otto could not quite make out, the sun glinting off of the sides of it.

In a moment of realisation, Otto's heart seemed almost to implode, and his stomach tumble. There were four Russians, and their uniforms were unlike that of the foot soldiers which the crew had seen at the village previously. They were the uniforms of a Soviet tank crew. They had run to a green metallic structure, which seemed to dwarf the T-34 for size, perhaps explaining why Otto did not make such a connection in the first instance. But before he could cry out to Greim that there was an enemy tank on their flank, one of the town hall's supporting pillars exploded into a cloud of rubble, as a shell ripped it in two. The projectile narrowly missed the Tiger, flying a foot above the turret and crashing into the building next to them, littering the Panzer with a shower of debris.

"Hostile tank! Evasive action, move, move!" yelled Greim through the intercom, as Scholl frantically rotated the turret towards their aggressor. Otto spun the tracks to angle the Tiger's armour, with the Russian tank at their diagonal right, in order to provide the best chance of shots deflecting. A second shell flew from the cloud of brick dust, bouncing just in front of Otto's seat with a deep reverberating clang, and again striking the buildings to the left of the Tiger. The Soviet machine rolled into view now, and it was a beast. One of the most advanced and armoured Russian vehicles, the IS-2, was now moving towards the Tiger, providing a deadly challenge to the usual apex predatorial status enjoyed by the Tiger's crew. This was very different to the T-34s that Otto and his comrades usually fought against, which, while a capable enemy, would not individually tip the odds against the Tiger; no, this IS tank could very well spell the crew's doom.

Scholl managed to loose a shot once the turret had completed its traverse, yet this merely pinged upwards upon contact with the sloped Soviet turret, failing to bother the olive green giant. Otto pushed the Tiger's engine to its absolute limit, so desperate was he to get the crew to the comparative sanctuary of the rubble-ridden streets behind the town hall and away from the square, with their better cover. The Russian machine guns had started to pepper the Tiger with lead now, reminding each man of the immediate proximity of the danger facing them. Rounding the corner of the town hall, Otto heard another round zip past the Tiger, missing its rear by mere centimetres, and flying down the abandoned road.

With several turns and some difficult driving, Otto realised that he had temporarily broken the line of sight between the Russian and his own tank, and awaited Greim's instructions. Raeder was assisting Otto as a spotter, helping him avoid obstacles by peering out of his hatch when safe to do so.

Greim was his usual calm self, and eventually called, "Continue along this road, Griff. We need to try to find some sort of industrial area, some kind of factory or warehouse, in which we can manoeuvre more freely without being exposed."

And so, Otto carried onwards, taking a side road every now and then in order to not be spotted by the Russian tank which followed closely behind.

The Soviets were well aware of the Tiger's position, sighting it here and there as it turned a corner, escaping moments before their gun sight lined up with the German machine. Eventually, the crew discovered a large set of warehouses, presumably armament factories and storage, which they could use for a solace against the Russian bear. The issue, however, was that they would be exposed for too long in their dash for the entrance that they were bound to receive a shell in their back. Otto knew fully well that a hit from the rear would punch straight through the Tiger's armour, likely splintering and killing most, if not all, of the crew.

"What do we do now, Herr Hauptman?" yelled the driver, hoping for some miraculous solution.

Greim paused for a moment, and then asked, "Smoke shells, we still have one or two, right?" Kellerman nodded the affirmative, and so Greim continued. "Strap a grenade to it. We can throw it off the rear of the tank, which should provide just enough cover. Raeder, get to it!"

Otto turned the last corner, bringing the crew onto the final straight towards the factory. They had a matter of seconds before the Russian would be upon them, and so needed to act quickly. Kellerman handed Raeder the rigged smoke shell, who climbed quickly from the tank and dropped the device behind the Tiger, pulling the pin before retiring to his seat. The bang was followed by the whoosh of a smoke cloud, the entire shell having exploded, and providing ideal cover for the crew. The grey bubble arose steadily, covering the whole road behind the Panzer, and Otto used this short opportunity to power the Tiger into the warehouse and behind the maze of crates. It was fortunate, thought Otto, that the crew didn't have far to travel, for such wasteful driving would have otherwise drained them of fuel extremely quickly.

The crew were then presented with a maze of boxes and crates, a labyrinth of containers, most of which had been opened and looted, probably taken by the fleeing soldiers which passed through the town on account of their being short on ammunition. The Tiger was restricted in which routes it could take by its size, with only particular paths through the storage units being able to accommodate the width of the machine, lest they give away their position by crashing through the wooden stacks. Otto took the leftmost route through the enormous warehouse, rumbling along the winding passage. Through the gaps in the towering boxes, he could see the IS-2 burst through the smoke screen and zoom towards the warehouse in pursuit.

Now, it was cat and mouse. The Tiger was in the unusual position of prey, hiding as best as it could from the Soviet giant. So often the dominant hunter, from Seelow to the Steppe, the crew now needed to go on the defensive, and defeat this enemy by use of cunning, rather than simply rely on the Tiger's bite. For now, Otto continued to push their Panzer through the dimly lit annals of crates, until a plan could be devised. The intercom was silent, each man waiting for a sign that the enemy had them sighted. Otto could feel the sweat beading from his forehead, dripping down his nose and wetting his shirt. What the hell could they do against that thing? At moments like this, the young driver found great sympathy with Raeder's usual nervous self, fully understanding how the poor boy had got into such a state. However, what was particularly biting, is that Raeder had steeled himself since his fiery rescue and assault ingenuity, and so Otto was now, it seemed, the nervous one of the group.

Greim, after some time, broke the silence of the crew. "How are we going to do this, then?"

Otto was unnerved by the commander's uncertainty; it was unusual for Greim to need help in devising a battle plan, let alone to throw the question out to the crew. But Greim was nothing if not wise, and a wise man knew when to ask for help. A few moments of quiet passed, only coloured by the continuous revs of the Tiger's engine. Finally, Kellerman spoke up.

"If we could perhaps knock their tracks off, Herr Hauptman? At least we would have the advantage again?"

It was true that an immobile tank, even a mechanical monster such as the IS-2, was unable to command the battlefield. But how to do it? The crew would surely be blown to kingdom come if they sat in the enemy's line of sight for long enough to allow Scholl to take a bead on their caterpillar tracks.

"A landmine?" suggested Otto. He figured that if a landmine exploded outwards, it should cripple the enemy machine, as it had their Tiger on countless occasions.

"But the Soviets would mow down whoever went out to plant it, it can't be done," sighed Scholl. They needed to find some way of delivering the mine without exposing themselves from behind the Tiger's armour. Raeder suddenly slapped his hand on his thigh, and began to yell into the intercom.

"We can ram them!" he yelled. "If we put a little armour on the front of the Tiger, just a few centimetres sheet, we can put the landmine on there and ram the side of them!"

It was a risky business; the mine could knock off their own track in the process, or worse still it could penetrate the tank and kill the crew. But what choice did they have? If they didn't find a solution, the IS would spell their end regardless.

Having agreed on the delivery mechanism, they now needed to figure out how to implement it. They would need to find a way to sneak up on the enemy tank, so close as to ram their side, and then prevent their counterattacking. It was now Scholl who would innovate for the group.

"They followed the smoke screen," he said, deep in thought. "I see no reason they wouldn't do so again. If we fire our last smoke shell, then hide amidst the crates and power down, they should come right near, thinking we have carried on. If we hit their side and stay close, they won't be able to turn their gun on us, it'll only get stuck on the side of our turret," he explained.

Again, this plan seemed the only option currently available to the crew. And so, when they reached the next straight point, at the warehouse's perimeter, Kellerman loaded a smoke shell into the cannon. This was fired at the Tiger's feet, and Otto hid the machine in the billowing cloud. He then reversed into the nearest row of crates, and Raeder jumped out to affix the landmine and armour to the Tiger's front. A spare line of caterpillar track was used to augment their frontal protection. Once this was completed, Otto turned off the engine, and the crew waited with bated breath. Due to the short time between switching the engine off and soon on, time required to reheat would be minimal, and it should jump back into life almost instantly. Otto only hoped that it wouldn't stall.

Raeder jumped back into his seat and closed his hatch in silence. Now, all that remained was to see if their opponent took the bait.

"Come on, come on!" whispered Kellerman under his breath; if the Soviet tank chose instead to flank the smoke cloud, it would see the hole which the Tiger had smashed in the crates as it hid itself, and surely destroy it. Otto glued his eyes to his periscope sight, scanning the grey mist which surrounded the crew, waiting for its being broken. A distant engine rumble and squeaking of tracks was becoming steadily more audible, as the enemy tank moved closer. But was it approaching the smoke screen, or flanking the Panzer? From the metallic hull, such reverberation was almost inaudible, and it was impossible to pin the exact location of its source.

Finally, after what seemed to Otto to be an eternity of waiting, with the engine hum of the IS-2 growing to deafening levels, the smoke in front of the Tiger became occupied with a shadow. Otto could see the enormous green hulk pass in front of their own machine, moving extremely slowly and cautiously, hearing the turret rotate back and forth as it searched for its potential prey. The smoke washed over its tremendous frame, and it had not quite spotted the Tiger buried amidst the crates, waiting to pounce. Otto waited for the customary connection of Greim's foot on his shoulder, signalling his need to launch the Tiger forwards into the enemy's side. He prayed that Raeder had managed to mount the anti-tank mine at the right angle and height to disable the enemy track in one blow.

Finally, feeling Greim's boot in his back, Otto brought the Tiger to life. The engine growled instantly, ready to strike the beast which stood before it. He revved the throttle, and the machine jumped violently forward. The Tiger contacted the IS-2, jolting all of the crew forward, with Otto narrowly avoiding hitting his head on the Panzer's armour. The landmine detonated with an almighty prang, and Otto heard with great relief the rattle of a thrown track, showing that the attack had done its job. What then passed was a moment of confusion; what did they do now? The Russian crew could be heard yelling at one another in confusion, while the Tiger remained quiet, hoping to work out how to now destroy the enemy they had disabled.

Greim barked an order after a number of seconds, commanding, "Out of the tank!"

Opening his hatch, Otto jumped to the roof of the Tiger, swinging his MP40 from his back. The smoke was still thick, and so it was difficult for him to make out any figures approaching. He leapt to the enemy tank, his boots tapping on the thick metal hull, watching the enemy hatches for any sign of movement. The rest of the crew had also opened hatches, with Raeder having followed Otto atop the enemy tank. Moving towards the enemy turret, Otto was checking the hatches, which seemed to be closed. But what was that darkness behind the turret, some sort of crouching figure perhaps?

Before Otto had time to cock and aim his MP40, the figure pounced from his spot behind the turret and crashed into Otto. From the smoke had emerged an incredibly muscular Russian tanker, who grabbed Otto by the collar and launched him from the roof of the IS-2 with a grunt. He fell to the dirty concrete floor of the warehouse with a thud, his side ringing with pain, and having had the air knocked from him. The Russian jumped from the roof, as Otto frantically searched for his weapon which had been knocked from his hand on impact. The Soviet yelled as he approached Otto, who tried to avoid his kicks. Otto rolled as he dodged attacks from the Russian, who then jumped on him and began punching his face, teeth bared. This was bad; Otto was reminded of the Russian who had accompanied Alexei back at the cottage and strangled him, and knew he had to escape. The Soviet was now pulling Otto by the collar and trying to smash his head onto the concrete, as Otto attempted to block or avoid the worst of the blows.

The man's hot breath and spit was spreading across Otto's face as he continued his assault, and Otto was starting to run short of energy with which to resist his punches and grapples. However, as he tried in vain to push the Russian's side to reduce his balance, he noticed a holster on his belt. A knife perhaps? His fingers fumbled in desperation to find its contents, his other arm still trying to block the Soviet's blows, which were now starting to land with serious pain upon Otto's jaw and cheek. Finally, the cover of the holster had come loose, and Otto realised with delight that it was in fact a pistol. He had taken the weapon from the belt but would now need to break the enemy's iron grip for long enough to angle the pistol into his attacker's body.

The Russian was still growling furiously and managed to crack Otto's head lightly against the ground. His vision blurred for a moment; he felt quite sick at the hit and was beginning to panic. There would have been no use in retrieving the pistol if he was simply to be knocked out or killed before he could utilise such a find. His mouth was filled with a metallic taste, as blood leaked from Otto's lips following the Russian's punches, which provided Otto with a dawning revelation. That was it! He brough his face closer to the Russian's, in between his head being repeatedly thrown to the floor, and spat some of the blood which had gathered in his mouth, landing most of it in his enemy's eyes. It provided just enough of a loosening of grip, as the man pulled away for a moment, blinking with pain as he attempted to clear his eyes of Otto's blood. This allowed Otto to ready the pistol, and he fired into the Russian's stomach. The man tensed and winced with a growl, still not releasing Otto. Emptying the entire magazine into the Russian in panic, Otto jolted with each shot, the powerful pistol creating no small amount of recoil.

With all shots emptied, the Soviet loosened his grip, Otto's stomach turning warm as it became drenched in the Russian's own blood leaking across it. He let out a small gurgle, his death rattle finally signalling to Otto that he could regain his nerve, and he pushed the Russian off of him. Standing, and attempting to recover from such a savage beating, Otto scanned the still-thick smoke for either his MP40 or another opponent. What was going on around him? He heard yelling, the odd shot fired in the mist, and grunts of crewmen locked in melee combat. Otto continued to scan the smoke around him, hoping to assist his fellow crewmembers.

He was soon surprised when yet another figure emerged from the smoke, charging at Otto. His uniform revealed him to be a Russian, and he was sprinting towards Otto with arms outstretched. Shocked at the appearance of a second aggressor, Otto simply began to run as fast as he could, Soviet soldier in pursuit, blasting through the smoke screen and along the rows of crates. Winding through the maze, he was beginning to gain some distance from his follower; his upper body strength had been totally drained in his scrap with the first Russian, and he would surely lose a fight with this second attacker. He continued to sprint, his chest aching with the strain and lactic acid pumping through his veins as he continued to craft as random a route as possible through the stacked boxes of the warehouse.

His legs were hurting terribly, and he knew that he would

be forced to bring this chase to an end soon. While he could outdo his pursuer for speed, he could know nothing about the man's levels of endurance. Bringing his route to a full circle, he began moving back towards the two interlocked tanks. The sounds of fighting had died down by now, and it sounded that one crew had just about finished off the other; he could only hope that his own comrades were victorious. The smoke cloud was dissipating, with only the centre remaining so opaque as to render the other side invisible. Otto noticed as he continued running towards the point from where he had started his retreat, that his MP40 was now visible, on the ground where he must have dropped it when thrown from the tank. As he arrived, he grabbed it from the floor and, a few steps on, turned to face his enemy.

In those few steps, however, it seemed that he had continued into the thickest section of the smoke screen and could no longer see his opponent. He had two choices, and perhaps a few seconds to decide which to take. The first option would be to wait until he sighted the enemy darken the smoke in front of him, and to then send a well-aimed burst into him. The advantages of this approach were obvious; there would be less wasted shots, and the accurate nature of his counter would have a higher chance of instantly incapacitating his assailant. However, there was a high chance that if the Russian came from an angle at which Otto was not aiming, he would not be able to correct his weapon in time, be knocked to the ground, and likely killed in the ensuing melee by virtue of his exhausted state. The second option was to start firing wildly in the possible direction of the Russian. If he hit the enemy soldier, he would have solved his problem immediately, assuming the shot was critical enough to fell his enemy. On the other hand, of course, if he were to miss his enemy, the result would be the same as a failure of his first option.

In the moment it had taken him to evaluate these options, he realised that the second approach seemed the option with the highest chance of success; the thirty-two shots of his MP40 should cover a decent area, and hopefully at least a few of them should hit their target. With that, Otto began spraying bullets left and right, covering about forty-five degrees in the direction from which he was being chased. The bullets tore holes in the smoke cloud, zipping through the air in all directions. Otto continued to fire until he was out of ammunition, the clacking of his submachine gun signalling an empty magazine. Now, it was only to be hoped that his shots had indeed landed, as he loaded his second magazine. If he had failed, he would soon be confronted by the still-attacking Russian. However, with the burst of his weapon being proceeded by silence, he soon heard a slump of a falling body ahead of him.

MP40 cocked and readied, Otto cautiously stepped from the ever-decreasing smoke, and caught sight of the outline of a body strewn across the floor. The man had fallen to the side, likely having stumbled as he tried to continue his run amidst a hail of lead. Judging by the blood stream across the floor, it seemed that Otto had landed four shots on the Soviet chaser, the first shot hitting him around ten metres from his falling point. The man had continued for a short time before being hit by the other three bullets, stumbling to his knees, and then falling onto his side. He was dead before Otto had arrived at his corpse, the emotionless eyes staring up at the partially translucent roof, his mouth open, and his arm still clutching at one of his bullet holes. One shot, presumably the first, had entered his shoulder, which would have enabled the man's adrenaline to continue carrying him forward. The next three had hit the man first in the stomach, then two in the upper chest just below his neck. A pool of blood was expanding steadily around the cadaver, connecting with the thickening streak left from where he had run.

Death seemed to be bothering Otto increasingly less. In these past few days, he had been confronted with an unprecedented increase in his encounters with death while outside the protective armour of the Tiger, which had always seemed to provide a barrier between him and the destruction which he caused. But now that he had become accustomed to the writhing pain and death rattles of those around him, it haunted him less and less, perhaps due to his mantra of not thinking about it becoming so ingrained as to be almost automatic. The only face which still truly haunted Otto was that of brave Alexei, his confrontation with eternity being so brave and forthright, retaining his human dignity right to the last breath. Otto fingered the blood-stained letter of Alexei's which still lay crumpled in his pocket, curious as to what its contents might read, and still mindful to pass it on to someone, eventually going to his sweetheart back in the Soviet Union.

He returned to the Tiger, remembering that he hadn't checked as to the success of his crew against the enemy. He hoped that as he had defeated two of the four Russians, the remaining four of the German crew would be able to take the other two with ease. The smoke had all but dissipated by now, and he sighted Kellerman and Scholl sitting exhaustedly upon the turret of the Tiger.

"Don't worry, Greim and Raeder are just searching the body of the Russian commander. We managed to finish the others, and our own track wasn't thrown; all in all, a successful attack!" reported Kellerman, amidst gasps and sips of water, as he regained his breath.

The blood stains coating the arms of his tunic seemed to match the amount lost by the mangled corpse, which had its head smashed several times upon the gun of the Soviet IS-2 tank. It looked to have been an incredibly violent death, with crimson stains covering most of the IS-2's roof, explaining Kellerman's exhaustion. The loader seemed totally undisturbed at having wrestled life from his Russian counterpart with his bare hands, so saturated was he with the horrors of war. Otto joined the pair, and they sat in silence as they recovered. They all felt that death was their new crew member, so often had they brushed with him, and now a near ending experience was almost routine. Kellerman had lit his pipe, Scholl was staring tiredly into the middle distance, and Otto simply regained his breath. After some time, Greim rounded the corner, and congratulated Otto on his elimination of two of the enemy crewmen.

"It was worth it though!" exclaimed Raeder, proudly waving a scrap of paper aloft, presumably recovered from the Russian tank commander. "This shows that there should be no more enemy positions between us and Berlin! We are about an hour away, with two hours to cover the distance before the next attack is due," he grinned.

However, the crew did not share in his excitement. They knew that getting to Berlin would actually achieve very little in the way of their long-term survivability. They still wished to get to the city, if only to continue normality for a few days longer. And that way, however the war ended, they would at least know what to do with themselves after, or more likely, die fighting. They simply stood, remounted their faithful Tiger, and prepared to move off once more. Otto restarted the engine, reversed from the emptied husk of the once-feared IS-2, and moved through to the other side of the warehouse. Raeder's enthusiasm was touching to the more experienced other crew members. It reminded Otto of himself in early 1942; new to the Wehrmacht, and excited to participate in the lightning victories of 1940 and 1941, riding the hubris generated by the tales he was told in training of German columns breezing through poor defences. The grinding attrition of Stalingrad, the crushing defeats in Operation Bagration, these were all yet to come, and he retained at that time a naïve innocence such as that purported by Raeder.

Otto was also growing nervous. What scenes would he discover in his former childhood home? That city which had been full of such wonder and history, which had been the beating heart of Otto's proud German Reich; a Reich which he had become steadily disillusioned with as it continued morally spiralling. If he was honest with himself, Otto knew that the only real reason he hadn't deserted already was his loyalty to his own crew, and Greim's military traditionalism wouldn't allow such actions. Greim was curious in his devotion to such a defunct regime; the man was clearly no National Socialist, nor were any of the crew anymore, yet his family's proud history in Germany's, and formerly Prussia's, armies, required his absolute obedience to his country. This also helped to explain the man's deep-set hatred towards the SS, who he regarded as thoroughly unsoldierly.

Raeder, despite his age, was also far from a Nazi, but more a boy excited to be in a uniform and broken by war. He recently steeled his nerves, yet a revert to his former self would likely occur when they reached the urban combat of Berlin, and so Otto made a mental note to keep a careful eye on the boy. Kellerman was an old warrior, and frankly seemed to care little for politics; a true hunter, he simply knew to carry on loading, and deal with the implications of the war at some later date which he would indefinitely postpone. And finally, Scholl only wanted to maintain the morale of his friends which surrounded him, and had often been a vital shoulder to lean on when Otto was constantly stressed on the front. But the mismatch of a crew always seemed to work so well together, and so on they travelled, ever closer to besieged Berlin.

Chapter 9
11.7 Kilometres From Berlin

The crew had largely cleared the urban foliage of the previous town by now and were covering the short handful of miles between the town and Berlin, which now stood easily visible before them. The crew could see defensive lines and structures caked in smoke, enjoying the brief – and likely final – pause in the fighting, as the Soviets were making ready for their last push. Armoured units would soon flood this dusty road along which the Tiger walked, as the Red pincers clamped down on the heart of the Reich. The measly fortifications would do little to break the waters of the iron tide the Soviets would unleash, and were more a token resistance offered by the paralysed German war machine, perhaps if only to convince the most oblivious onlooker that there was still hope. Though by this point, Otto thought, even a blind man would see that the result was a foregone conclusion.

The crew was busy soaking in the warm spring day, as they passed the last patches of blue sky before they were engulfed in the all-consuming smoke cloud which suffocated the capital. With his head out of the driver's hatch, Otto was leisurely steering the Tiger down the winding country trail, spotting birds flitting as though they were angels between the deeply green trees. Their surroundings were a mixture of tall-grassed fields and the odd woodland thicket, soon to be choked by the grey rubble of Berlin's boundaries. But for the moment, Otto joined his colleagues in admiring the nature which enveloped their vision and tried to ignore any preconceptions on what they would see when they arrived.

"How are you faring, boys?" inquired Greim. The crew had been relatively silent since their clash with the IS-2, and Greim would not consider himself to be fulfilling his duties if he didn't take this quiet opportunity to survey the mental state of his men. In more normal circumstances, he might have done this around the campfire or back at base, but respite had been thin on the grounds in the past weeks.

"Oh, about as well as I can be when I have to be stuck in a metal box with Kellerman's smell," jeered Scholl, who had seemed revived by the idyllic country road, and resumed his usual hijinks. Kellerman gave him a quick clip on the ear, and the whole crew managed to find a chuckle left in them.

"I'm doing all right, Herr Hauptman," replied Otto. He had shaken off the adrenaline from dodging the two burly Russian tankers, and realised quite what a brush with eternity that was for him. If for a change so small as the first assailant's pistol not being readily cocked, Otto's brains would have doubtless been dashed across the floor of the warehouse. But he was simply choosing to ignore it and focus as best he could on the here and now; he was driving quietly down a country road with what were essentially his family, and it could be worse.

"What about you, Raeder?" asked Greim.

The boy smiled back to his commander, replying, "I'll be fine as long as you don't make me jump into fire again!" Hans Raeder had seemed to finally gain the necessary insanity to keep going in this war, and much of his initial annoying –

though completely understandable – nerves had left him. Kellerman had almost grown proud of the young lad, feeling that his persistent harshness had somehow moulded him into a soldier. As for Kellerman himself, he simply grunted the affirmative.

The late morning silence was soon broken by a sound which did not denote danger, but rather annoyance to the crew. A crunch could be heard, and the Panzer hunched forward. As much as Otto revved, there was no change except dust being kicked up from the furiously spinning caterpillar tracks; the Tiger was simply stuck in a ditch. The entire crew let out a simultaneous sigh, frustrated at having to fix this ridiculous issue once more. Thankfully, they carried a large log tied to the side armour of the tank, which could be wedged between the tracks and the ground to provide traction.

Kellerman and Raeder grudgingly arose from their seats, and exited the cabin, preparing to remove the log from its securing straps. Meanwhile, it was the task of the rest of the crew to watch carefully for threats; immobility heralded one of the most vulnerable moments for any tank, for an aggressor would be able to attack from whichever chosen angle, with their prey paralysed to dodge. An attack was unlikely when disabled by such a natural obstacle, rather than a pre-set landmine or the like, but there was always the possibility that a particularly perceptive soviet scout was watching the spot, should any strugglers such as themselves fall victim to the dip in the road. They scanned the treelines and grasses which surrounded their vehicle, his eyes peeled for any movement.

For now, however, all seemed tranquil. Kellerman and Raeder had readied the log, and were now setting about trying to jam it into place with entrenching tools. Greim had lowered himself back below his hatch, and was scanning the fields and bushes for hostiles. Otto, however, with his restricted driver's view, used this as a rare opportunity to retreat into his thoughts. And he could not wrench them away from Alexei's letter. What could it possibly say? These final prepared words for a loved one? But the thing that continued to chill Otto was Alexei's unusual acceptance of death, his enhanced perspective on the fate that was to befall him. He was so calm, so understanding of his passing, and so far from the animalistic messes usually seen coughing blood, fear-stricken eyes darting around for some impossible solution.

Otto's moment of self-reflection was interrupted by yet another metallic hollow clang, from outside the Tiger. While the noise was loud, it did not seem to speak of any real damage, with projectiles such as tank shells being easily ruled out. Whatever it was had been moving at some speed, however, with a whizzing as the projectile zipped through the air. What could it have been, this deepened ping which had reverberated through the cabin of the crew? Otto went to turn towards Greim, asking what the sound was, until it was paired with yet a further noise; a truly blood curdling scream.

It didn't take long for Otto's heart to almost stop as he realised from whence the scream had originated. Raeder. He looked out of his periscope to see the ground before the Tiger spattered with blood, while Kellerman crouched over their yelling comrade. It appeared that the clang had been a Soviet anti-tank round; it was more than hopeful for the Soviet to have believed that his rifle had a chance to penetrate the Tiger's frontal armour, but regardless the shell had bounced from the hull and torn through Raeder as he readied the log.

Before Otto could even think, Greim yelled to him,

"Drive! Now!"

This confused Otto as the tank was still stuck fast, but he followed his commander's advice and spun the tracks as quickly as he could. Predictably, the Tiger failed to free itself. Had Greim simply panicked?

Of course not. While the tank indeed failed to move, the dusty road kicked up an enormous cloud of thick beige dirt as the caterpillar tracks spun against it, until the tank had at least partial cover, even if only for a moment. It was, as usual, a superb reaction on Greim's part, and he followed with a second order.

"Out the tank! Left side!"

Otto and Scholl followed accordingly, diving to the dry ground on the left side of the vehicle. As Raeder was on the left of the tank, the fact that the shot had deflected towards him proved that their attacker was to their right. Moments later they were joined by Greim, who had quickly grabbed his hunting rifle from the tank, and now sat with them next to the side of the vehicle.

Raeder's health was in a bad way. The bullet had hit the poor lad in his mid-thigh and shattered the bone. The rest of the leg had been practically blown off, with only a few inches of flesh keeping it attached. Tendons and broken bone were visible though the waves of blood, and Raeder could not stop screaming. It was a horrible state to see anyone in, let alone a dear friend. Kellerman in particular was crying, his usual gruff personality having being replaced with utter shock at this sight. A crimson trail showed that Raeder had been dragged, likely with no small measure of agony, from the front to the side of the tank, and was now clutching desperately to block the gaping injury. Kellerman was holding Raeder's hand and trying to fortify his resolve, while Scholl was busy applying a tourniquet to the upper thigh in an attempt to restrict the blood flow.

Otto felt frozen in the image of his friend. This poor boy, who should have been running for the Munich athletic team at this age, was laying before them in the utmost pain and fear. He had only just accustomed to war, a task that many soldiers never accomplished, and had suddenly been ripped through by a rogue bullet. The high calibre of the Soviet AT round meant that his injury was far beyond what most of the men could ever expect from a shot, and despite Scholl's best efforts, blood continued to seep through and soak the bandages. His uniform was turning a deep purple as it became saturated, and his face portrayed a ghostly pale.

Otto's dumbstruck state was only broken when Greim grabbed his shoulder, instructing him to follow into the long grass parallel to the tank. The pair dived in and crawled until they had cleared at least a hundred yards from the Panzer and their critically wounded colleague. Greim had readied his rifle and was scanning a distant treeline from which he suspected the shot had originated. Otto, however, could not take his eyes away from the Tiger through the tall spring grass, Raeder's cries still blood-chillingly audible from the other side. Seconds before, the world had been so tranquil, so calm. And in a blink, Raeder had been split in half by a chance shot, and the entire crew had been forced to leap into action. It seemed to Otto that the closer that they got to Berlin, the more that nature was steadily conquered by the war, that the delicate dichotomy between creation and destruction tipped further towards the latter. No calmness was ever truly safe anymore.

Greim, spying Otto's dwelling on the condition his poor

friend had been reduced to, patted his side in an attempt to snap him out of it. He gestured for Otto to crawl forward to a small ridge, perhaps half a foot higher, to get a slightly better vantage point of their target, and indeed to distract Otto with a task. As he shuffled along the rocky and uneven field, careful not to raise his head any more than necessary and present a choice shot for his enemy, Otto realised quite how physically exhausted he was. Sitting at the Tiger's driver seat, his tiredness had been masked to some extent, and when he had been forced to labour outside the tank such as at the outpost or when attacking the enemy IS-2, the adrenaline coursing through his veins had allowed him to feign a level of energy even to himself.

But now, as he dragged himself through the dusty and uncomfortable field, his true unmanipulated degree of exhaustion was laid before him bare. All of his muscles ached terribly, straining and tearing as he hauled his carcass forward. He was covered by cuts, bruises, abrasions and chafes, which burned as his scratchy uniform rubbed against him. Otto was also half starved, having eaten rather little in the past days, and this had only exacerbated his weakness. His mouth, too, was like cotton, and his thirst combined with the heat of the day, which was far greater than when the Tiger's movement had provided some wind, to concoct a pounding headache.

His uniform did not seem to be coping any better than its flesh inhabitant. His tunic, shirt, and trousers were all covered in tears and holes, and had hardened in places with the salt in Otto's sweat. The freshness gained when their apparel had been washed at Herr Sichter's had totally disappeared, and instead his clothes were swarmed by the stench of body odour, grease, and blood. His collar was speckled with his own dried blood, and his lower front covered with that of his enemies. Otto's boots were breaking at the seams, and his feet had moved beyond mere blisters to weeping sores, with the soles caked in dried mud. But still, the wounded and weary driver crawled onwards, until he had reached the small rise in the field.

Looking back at Greim, Otto awaited instructions. Scholl seemed desperate to help, but dared not step from the shelter of the Tiger's side, and so stayed with Kellerman and Raeder. Raeder had quietened now, but was still groaning and moaning.

Greim signalled Otto to keep an eye on the treeline, whispering, "Let's see if he fancies a bit of bait!"

Slowly, the commander lifted his officer's cap off, which he often deigned to wear instead of the standard smaller Panzer cap and raised it carefully just above the grasses. Sure enough, Otto caught a flash out of the corner of his eye, roughly thirty degrees to the right of where the pair were facing. Milliseconds later, a crack sounded across the field, and Greim's hat flew out of his hand as a bullet smacked into it, prompting him to bury his face in the mud quickly.

"He is a keen shot," observed Otto, as Greim collected himself, and replaced his cap upon his head, now accessorised with a bullet hole in the front right.

"True enough," he replied, and worked the action on his rifle.

It was a beautiful lever-action piece, exquisitely engraved and bearing a large calibre. Greim had been a practiced hunter in peacetime, and as such he was used to stalking prey in this fashion. He followed Otto's line of sight to where the shot had originated and used his binoculars to spot a small observation platform on the edge of the forest, a few hundred yards from their current position.

"I'll try for the platform, and then we will need to test if he is still alive. If we don't, he will kill us before we can displace." Something in Greim's tone worried Otto, who was pretty sure that the test as to whether the Russian was still breathing would involve an Otto-shaped bait.

After some scope adjustments and testing for wind and distance, Greim was ready to fire. "As soon as I fire, you need to stand up, then drop down whether there is a shot or not. Based on his accuracy and speed, he will fire in that time if he survives, and we need to be sure he doesn't follow my muzzle flash. Don't try to rely on your reactions to get you back on the floor in time, don't wait to see a shot, just drop down," he told Otto. This was not going to be fun. Otto took some deep breaths, hoping to God that Greim's bullet would strike home. And he waited.

Finally, Greim's shot rang through Otto's ears, and he knew what to do. He pushed himself up off of the ground from his front, aiming to simply tip and fall onto his back. Just as he began to fall backwards, he noticed yet another flash from the treeline. A bullet zipped past, inches from Otto's face as he fell backwards, followed by the crackle of his opponent's rifle. The Russian was still alive, but Otto was simply overjoyed that he remained so himself. That was unsettlingly close, he thought. Cursing, Greim prepared to dive away, yelling to Otto that the pair needed to evacuate.

"Displace! Move, boy!"

They moved sideways, and another bullet sailed past them, lower this time, zooming through the long grass and burying itself with a small cloud of dust behind them.

After they had crawled a few more yards, sufficient to hide themselves, Greim handed Otto the binoculars to try and find their enemy. In the next few minutes, two more shots raced close past Otto's position. It seemed that Otto had rather foolishly managed to maroon himself between two tractor marks in the field, and so was unable to move; if he tried to crawl further, or indeed jump and fall again, the Russian would know his exact location. He realised this as Greim handed him the binoculars across the track mark, and that Greim was able to access the rest of the field while Otto couldn't.

"Damn it, Griff, why did you stop there!" snapped Greim, frustrated at his ally's subsequent inability to move further. His anger was alleviated, however, when Otto told him what he had spotted; the Russian sniper, sitting at the treeline and waiting for his targets to reveal themselves. "Right, you'll have to shoot him," said Greim. "I'm blocked by a ridge, and if you try to distract him he will kill you, as you can't move."

Otto, who had never hunted, let alone sniped, before, was practically hyperventilating. "How do I hit him?" he asked Greim with a panicked tone.

"Get a grip man. We will wait for a while, for him to tire of concentrating, and then I'll distract him. Just aim high, around the hundred and fifty-yard mark. There is little wind, and so shoot slightly to the left." This crash course in sniping seemed insufficient to teach Otto to be an expert marksman, but if this war had taught him one useful skill it was adaptability.

The pair now had to but wait for the Russian to lose enough focus to provide a few crucial seconds of readjustment when they chose to engage. If Otto shot now, and missed, the lack of distraction would lead to an immediate response from his enemy, and Otto's subsequent demise. It should only take a few minutes for total concentration and controlled breathing to grate on their opponent long enough to buy a second or two.

"Don't worry about Raeder," said Greim, who had noticed Otto periodically glancing back in the direction of the Tiger.

"I know, 'don't think about it'," said Otto, quoting his own well used mantra.

"I didn't say that," replied Greim, despondently.

"But that hides the insanity, no? Surely it's the only way to keep functioning?" replied Otto.

Greim simply sighed and shook his head. "If you only ever take one piece of advice from me boy, make it this one. This war, this God forsaken hell, was started by too many men telling themselves 'don't think about it'. Think about it for Christ's sake, or you will be doomed to repeat it."

Otto had never even considered this. Ignoring the insanity as to provide reason to carry on was pointless; there was no reason. The war was insane. It couldn't be reasoned with, it was a force at this point, a storm of iron and steel tide, sweeping away nature and logic, devolving mankind into its lowest stance. Carry on for your crew, sure, or because you've no other option. But stop trying to rationalise the irrational.

After a few minutes, it was time for Otto to ready his shot. He cycled the spent shell left by Greim in the chamber and closed the lever action. It was a remarkably well-weighted rifle, sitting comfortably and easily in Otto's inexperienced hands. Both the wood and metalwork were exquisitely engraved, with extensive patterns and the initials 'A.G.'. This may have been the initials of Greim's father, for the weapon was certainly decades old, yet extremely well maintained when one considered the hellish war through which it had been dragged. The scope atop the weapon appears to have been added later, not unlike the sights which Otto had seen affixed to the handguard of German snipers' Kar98s. It was, however, marked with several ranges at hundred-yard intervals.

"Right, control your breathing, boy," advised Greim, his eyes fixed on their target. "He is searching for us; I'll get up when he looks away."

"Do I hold my breath, Herr Hauptman?" asked a panicked Otto.

"No, breathe slowly and normally. When you want to fire, empty your lungs to two thirds' capacity and hold it just as you shoot; that will level your sights in between where your breathing has swayed. If you empty them completely, your sights will drop too far."

"Right, I'll give it my best." This was a lot for Otto to take in without prior training, but he was well aware that if he messed up the shot then Greim's distraction could well get the commander killed.

Otto levelled his sights and calmed his breathing as best he could. The Russian sniper was visible in the scope, and Otto pulled the crosshairs onto him. He adjusted for distance and wind, as Greim had told him. His enemy was wearing an ushanka hat, and bearing a Mosin-Nagant rifle, as he scoured the yellowed grasses ahead of him.

Greim dropped the binoculars and whispered to Otto, "Get ready. He is searching our right; he thinks we have crawled in the last few minutes. I'll hop up to draw his attention, fire as soon as you can."

Otto felt his heart thumping through the earth on which he lay but tried his hardest to prevent his hands from trembling or his breathing from speeding up.

Greim pushed up from the ground, diving to his left and falling on the ground. This was enough to draw out their enemy; the Russian stood up hurriedly, pulling his scope to where he had seen the tall tank commander jump, trying to find him in the tall grass. The Soviet was clearly a skilled sniper, being confident that he could still land the shot when standing. This had doubled the size of Otto's target, and, following Greim's breathing advice, he dialled in his scope and squeezed the trigger. The rifle had a tremendous recoil, striking Otto's shoulder with a great velocity, as the bullet was thrown forwards. There was a moment of anticipation, and then the Russian could be seen falling over, knocked down with no small amount of force.

Both men sprang into action. The enemy had definitely fallen, and they now had to close in on him before, if he was still alive, he collected himself and fired at them again. Greim pushed himself from the floor, unshaken by his dangerous dive in the face of an enemy marksman, with Otto following close behind as they waded through the tall golden stalks of grass. Greim had drawn his Luger P08, and kept the pistol aimed at the spot they had seen their enemy fall as they stepped through the field. As they ran, they made as much an effort as possible to keep low while not losing speed, to provide perhaps even a minor advantage to avoid any incoming shot, although Otto knew full well that this would do little to protect them.

As they reached the edge of the field, they found the Soviet propped against a tree. There was a great deal of blood painted in a trail leading a few metres to him, at the end of which was the discarded and blood-spattered rifle. The man had then dragged himself across the floor to the tree, with no small degree of pain. Otto's shot had struck the upper right chest, piercing the lung and passing through the Soviet's back, according to the crimson explosion on the ground. Reaching the tree, it seemed the Soviet had reached for his first aid kit in shock, but had passed away before he was able to utilise it; the soldier lay lifeless against the trunk, unravelled bandage in the opposite hand from his wound, and his other arm tucked into his side in some attempt to stem the blood flow. His eyes were staring into the middle distance, and blackish-red liquid was oozing from both the wound and his mouth, no longer spraying but simply exiting the man in a residual dribble. His face, still a picture of shock, was left motionless, as his head lulled to his side.

This was no time to admire Otto's marksmanship or lament the passing of a fellow warrior. They needed to come to Raeder's aid as quickly as possible. Greim unloaded a pistol shot into the Russian's torso to test he was dead, which passed through the corpse without eliciting a reaction, while Otto snatched the bandage from his hand, and the pair proceeded to sprint back towards the Tiger. They could no longer hear Raeder's groans, who Otto figured must have either passed unconscious or been plied with morphine in order to minimise his suffering. As they closed in on the tank however, they saw an unusual sight; Scholl was squatting a few metres from the vehicle, smoking a cigarette. Had they been able, Otto wandered, to quell the bleeding to such an extent that the boy now needed only rest?

But as they rounded the corner of the Tiger's hull, a horrific sight met their eyes. The entire floor was caked in blood to an extent which Otto had never before seen, some a dried purplish brown, and some a burning red. Raeder lay in the middle of the pool of gore, his leg removed and lain next to him, while Kellerman sat over him holding his hand. The young boy seemed strangely pale and still for someone who only required one attendant to care for him?

But of course, Otto realised, with mounting horror, the fate which had befallen his young comrade. Kellerman's tears, so rarely wrought, were flowing plentifully down his cheeks as he desperately tried to wake the boy up, in denial of the state of his friend.

"We did all we could," reported Scholl, his voice awash with resignation and regret. "The bleeding wouldn't stop, even after we took the rest of the leg off. We gave him morphine; he went painlessly enough in the end," he said, choked up at the loss of his patient. Kellerman was crying dreadfully at the loss of this young man, who he had almost seen as a second son. The old war horse was unable to stomach the loss of yet another young son, real or imagined, and simply couldn't accept that he was gone.

Raeder's bloodied stump was torn viciously, while the rest of the leg which had been removed midway down the thigh lay next to him. Raeder looked incredibly peaceful, his eyes closed and one arm rested carefully on his chest, the other hand still held by a tearful Kellerman. His mouth was closed, and the young soldier looked almost asleep. The poor radioman, only recently turned soldier, had been caught by a stray bullet, and snuffed out just like that. Otto was particularly regretful that he wasn't present at his passing; could he have helped at all? Even if only to comfort him against eternity?

Scholl moved to Kellerman and crouched next to him, trying to pull his friend away from their fallen comrade.

"He's gone, Isaac. He's gone, leave him be," he said softly, patting Kellerman's shoulder. After some time shaking his head, Kellerman stood and yelled into the sky, a primal outburst of rage, as he struggled to comprehend the loss of what he had come to consider his own child. It's true that Kellerman had often been harsh with Raeder, but this was simply a matter of care; the battle-tested Kellerman was well aware of how unforgiving this war could be, and didn't want Raeder's inexperience to spell his downfall. He had always kept a close eye on the wellbeing of Raeder, and wanted the boy to survive this damned mess; Otto was convinced that Kellerman would gladly have given his life for the young man. Kellerman had not even been as upset at the loss of their former radio operator, Hermann Baum, with whom he had been close friends.

Greim also stormed away, stopping at the edge of the field and staring out in contemplation. While Greim would never display the warmth of their previous commander Von Stoltz, it clearly hurt him deeply losing anyone on his watch. Greim would, Otto was certain, suffer the most painful of deaths in order to save any man under his watch from coming to harm. His regimental way of holding himself, and meticulous mentality, did not cope well with emotional losses such as this, and he retreated into the tank to ponder.

"We won't even have time to bury him," sighed Otto. "If we do, we will miss our window into Berlin, and all end up the same." Kellerman, hearing Otto's bleak yet true assessment of the situation, gave a look as if he was about to shoot him.

"We bury him, all right! You damned dog, we bury him or I bury you!" snapped Kellerman, through waves of crying. Otto, knowing how upset Kellerman was, chose not to take this attack to heart. He glanced at Scholl, hoping that he would help to convince Kellerman of the necessities of the situation.

Before Scholl had a chance to even open his mouth, however, a deep and mighty boom erupted from next to the group, causing the three to drop to the floor in panic.

Looking up, they realised that the Tiger's cannon had sounded that mighty roar, and buried an explosive shell into the neighbouring field, tearing up earth several feet deep. Greim then opened the gunner's hatch, and announced to the cowering group: "The boy deserves a soldier's burial, and the Tiger should dig it for him. Bury him with dignity."

The group needed no second order; Kellerman and Otto lifted Raeder's limp cadaver carefully to the centre of the crater, replacing his hands on his chest and fastening the top buttons of his tunic. Scholl retrieved the leg and placed it below the severing point. They began gathering the thrown-out soil, and Greim dismounted the Panzer to join them.

He walked to the boy lain on the floor, and placed his rifle in Raeder's hands. "A true warrior deserves a true companion. This rifle has guarded my father and I for many a decade; I hope it is worthy for such a soldier of kind and true spirit as Raeder," he announced.

The eulogy had Kellerman in tears yet again, and the group lay a Zeltbahn over the body of their departed friend, and began collecting the soil back towards him. The help of the Tiger made the burial a quick business, taking no more than ten minutes, and they soon had the body covered with the earth.

Once the actual task of getting out of the ditch had been completed, the crew set off once more for Berlin, aware that this tragic spot would be their last stop. Otto felt almost glad that the innocent Raeder would not have to experience the horrors ahead, yet was torn with duality of thanking his rest and dearly missing his friend. The crew was deadly silent, as they approached their final maelstrom in Berlin, devoid of their comrade, and well aware that the city ahead would likely claim yet more of their small family as they struggled to defend this dying country which they could find few reasons to fight for. But, despite Greim's advice, only one thing would maintain sanity in insanity:

Don't think about it.

Chapter 10
2.3 Kilometres From Berlin

The crew, now only four strong, were continuing on their long and arduous road to Berlin. They had long passed Raeder's final resting place, which was now well out of sight, and were beginning to be enveloped by the sprawling concrete jungle that was Berlin. The defensive lines had drawn a short way inside the city, to utilise rubble and urban infrastructure for the futile resistance against the unstoppable Soviet hammer. The ghost of a once proud German capital now lay bare, preparing for the bloodshed it was about to host.

Former businesses, houses and community centres, police stations and hospitals, stood abandoned, their windows shattered and contents looted in the retreat. Empty café tables and bars, once filled with happiness and conversation, would soon be witness to a tremendous and terrible battle. Bullet casings, abandoned transports, and luggage littered the paved streets, crumpling under the tracks of the Tiger as it roared towards the city centre. The crew were unsure as to where they were expected to rendezvous, and so Otto simply continued towards the Reichstag in an attempt to contact the defenders. Artillery fire on the city was increasing in ferocity now, signalling the approaching attack, with certain stray shells falling close to the Tiger.

A palpable gloominess choked every man in the cabin. It

seemed impossible to Otto that the crew's proverbial child, the boy they had all tried to guide and nurture through the horrors which surrounded them, had been so brutally dispatched. Otto was both thankful that he had managed to avoid the twisted expressions and screams of pain undoubtably given by Raeder in his dying moments, yet regretted being forced to abandon his friend in the last minutes. He did not, however, feel any antipathy towards the Soviet sniper who had taken Raeder from them; having seen Greim pick off many an opponent in the last few months, Otto was well aware that if the tables had been turned, he would not have acted any differently.

The closer he got to Berlin, and the ever-increasing impossibility of the various tales of indestructibility as purported by German propaganda became clearer, Otto noticed that he was able to empathise with his opponents on a far more human level. The Soviet was no longer a barbaric uncivilised people, a subhuman animal which it was his moral duty to defend against; rather this 'Untermensch' revealed itself to be Otto's own equivalent in every way, simply trying to muddle through this God forsaken war. The Russians were defending their homeland and their people just as much as the Tiger's crew. While Otto was frankly unaware of the global consequences of the conflict, when it came down to each soldier, the insanity was inescapable.

This, perhaps, was the reason that Otto so wished he could translate Alexei's letter. The young soldier, what could his thoughts, so collected, have been at the eternity? He clearly had a sweetheart waiting for him, perhaps even children, and how long had it been since he had seen them? When would they find out that they would never see him again? And it was of course true that all the other Russians felled by the Tiger's crew were equally connected. Mothers' sons, children's fathers. And they were only the victims of this individual tank; when Otto thought about the number of people who had surely fallen on all sides, he almost grew faint at the enormity of life wasted.

Soon, however, his thoughts were interrupted, by the first men in German uniforms they had seen for some time, excepting Stefan Sichter and his rag-tag comrades. These men, however, were in little better condition. Half-starved, hollow faces, with torn uniforms and a strange assortment of weapons. The soldiers were a mixed bag, with some better-armed yet equally defeated SS men interspersed among the exhausted Wehrmacht remnants. The defenders were also joined by a worrying number of children, presumably Hitler Youth members, who lined the pitiful barricades and windows selected for defence. But no matter their age or experience, every man's expression portrayed one clear, deafening message: "I give up, get me out of here."

After a few minutes of passing the few and far between defensive positions, there came into view some officers gathered around a table in the centre of a crossroads. Upon the table sat a map of Berlin, and the men stood in silence around it, hoping to find a way of clawing some impossible victory from the jaws of defeat. Stopping the tank, the crew dismounted and approached the men.

Greim stepped forward, reporting, "Where do you need us, sir? We were split from the ninth army before the Battle of Halbe and made our way here."

The officer did not even look up, but simply waved them away, saying that they were to, "Go find Brigadeführer Krukenberg, with SS Panzer Division Nordland. He will find some use for you near Tiergarten."

"Is there anywhere we can pick up shells, fuel, or food?" inquired Greim, surprised at the officer's lack of direction. But the officer turned from the table, staring Greim down with a sneer.

"You think we have any to spare, let alone on a bunch of deserters?" he snapped.

Otto and Scholl, almost instinctively, had to restrain a still tearful Kellerman, who had begun to lunge towards the Officer. In response, the officer and his subordinates raised their weapons emotionlessly towards Kellerman, and they seemed about to fire. Greim, however, stepped between the officers and Kellerman, moving his chest in front of the gun barrels.

"Can you really afford to lose an experienced Tiger crew?" he demanded. Otto held his breath, fearing his commander was about to fall in an ill-considered martyrdom, or be made an example of. Thankfully, however, after a moment of unbearable tension, throughout which Otto dare not breathe, the officer lowered his pistol.

"Get out of here," he sighed, turning back to his map.

The crew needed no second reminder. Turning quickly, they remounted the battle-worn Panzer, and set off for Tiergarten. This required them to retreat into the 'Z', or 'Zentrum' (Centre) district, in order to find Krukenberg's headquarters. Greim heard from a passing defender that Krukenberg was head of the French SS 'Charlemagne' battalion and had been placed in further command of XI SS Panzergrenadier Division 'Nordland' to defend the northeast sectors of the city, having arrived from the west and been bolstered with Hungarian and Hitler Youth volunteers, as part of General Weidling's Berlin Defence Sector. It struck Otto that their own Tiger would likely be one of a very small handful of remaining German armour left in Berlin and would therefore have to bear the brunt of any counterattack.

By now, the artillery was falling all around them. Rubble explosions erupted across the streets, flinging dust and debris clanking across the Tiger's hull. What struck Otto, however, was that the Berlin population remained to be evacuated? Why, when all the other front city fortresses had been comprehensively cleared of civilians, had Hitler failed to take the same decision with Berlin? Men and women stumbled through the destruction in search of loved ones, while children looked for their parents in the ruins. Fires raged here and there, with critically undermanned and undersupplied defensive points desperately attempting to quell the worst of the flames and medically treat civilians and soldiers. The sound of battle was near and intense, heralding the beginning of the Russian attack. Through the hull reverberated the sounds of ripping machine gun fire, booming artillery, and rifles relentlessly cracking away.

The medical situation, too, was in shambles. Each small outpost was infested with doctors and nurses in bloodied aprons, rushing between row after row of wounded or recently dead soldiers. They were amputating and operating at frightful speed with little in the way of bandages, and all too often no anaesthetic. Screams and cries of injured men invaded the air, some from the medical tents, and some from areas of the street deemed too dangerous to mount a rescue from. Russian snipers had infiltrated many of the upper floors of buildings, and stole limbs from the troops below, often leaving them to bleed to death amid yells and cries, or even as they begged to be put out of their misery, yards away from their comrades. But bullets were precious, and minutes, or even hours, would pass before a seriously overworked Grim Reaper would pull them into eternity.

The position of bullet holes drilled into Volkssturm conscripts' bodies indicated that they had attempted to flee yet been gunned down by their own sides. The small number of streets briefly retaken from the Soviets showed scorch marks and shrapnel holes in the windows and cellars from where the Russians had neutralised Hitler Youth Panzerfaust operators, placed to ambush enemy armour. Otto felt almost as if this were imagined, some dreadful nightmare. Everything was falling apart. Even in the former retreats of the defeated Wehrmacht he had never encountered such disorder, such apocalyptic collapse. In the logical conclusion to his experience so far, madness had seized control; in an insane war, insanity finally ruled.

While the occasional small arms fire slammed into the side of the tank, the crew did not actually pass any significant breakthroughs exceeding local infantry offensives while they journeyed to Tiergarten. The battle raged in earnest by now, and they were sure to be required to combat Soviet armour with their pitiful handful of shells. Otto was amazed at the surreal nature of their surroundings, which was only exacerbated when a new model of German aircraft collided with the building to their front. While he had heard the stories of the purported 'Wunderwaffen' under development, he had found them about as palatable as stories of German superiority at this point. But through his drivers hatch he could clearly see a shot-down Me-262 jet propelled fighter, frankly striking him as a work of science fiction. Its crash, however, restrained the crew's amazement to the extent that none even thought it to be worthy of comment; the defeat of such a 'Wonder Weapon' over Berlin provided, Otto thought, a fitting representation of Germany's war hopes. The mightiest of machines, torn from the sky and hurled towards Berlin in a heap of flaming wreckage.

Families crossed the streets, holding onto children as they sought refuge from the fighting. Volkssturm units were harvested from the fleeing populace by black-clad SS officials, armed and pointed in the direction of the fiercest combat. They had perhaps minutes, Otto estimated, before they were cut down by Russian lead. The revving of the Tiger's engine did all it could to muffle the screams of agony, which still clawed their way through the hull, dragging themselves into the ears of the crew. Another explosion, closer now, ripped through the building perhaps fifty yards ahead of the Tiger. The boom was tremendous, causing the wall closest to the street to collapse across the road. Otto was uncertain as to whether the structure was hit by a piece of heavy artillery or an aircraft's bomb, but it had certainly put the road out of commission. Soldiers and civilians stumbled in the dust and smoke, spluttering as they regained their bearings, deafened by the blast.

"Damn. Carry us left, Griff, towards the Government Quarter. We shall have to cut through to Tiergarten," ordered Greim, frustrated at yet another delay.

Otto pulled the Tiger around the next turn, as the machine stalked the war-torn streets. They passed a large medical station, evidently recently struck by a large bomb, with the wounded stacked in droves. Line after line of dismembered bodies, screaming for help. The Russians were less than a block away, and these men saw little chance of receiving assistance. As they got closer to the Reichstag, however, they witnessed an even more heart wrenching sight.

SS soldiers were organising a new division of Volkssturm, untrained civilians simply told how to fire a weapon and sent to the front as cannon fodder. Boys as young as twelve, and men as old as seventy, were being torn from their families and pressed into the defence of the dying Reich. Many were not even being armed, so scarce was weaponry, but simply sent for 'assistance'. What hope did these people have of ever seeing their families again? Greim tapped Otto with his foot, signalling that he should stop the tank. As the Tiger screeched to a halt, the commander opened his hatch – an action not without risk in such a warzone – and questioned the lead SS officer.

"For what task are you arming these men, sir?" he asked.

The darkly uniformed man outranked Greim, and so he was forced to pay the SS the usual courtesies afforded to higher ranks. "They are to defend the north-eastern quarter. What of it?" asked the officer, outraged at the interruption of his sordid duty.

"They stand no chance against the Soviets; you must see that?" said Greim. "Did you not see action on the Eastern front?" he followed. The officer simply laughed with his squad members.

"Perhaps you wish to join them old man?" he chuckled, gesturing towards Greim with his pistol.

There was nothing the crew could do. Any act of protest and they would all be shot with impertinence. This was unlike the wooded clearing in which they had encountered Stefan Sichter and the Gauleiter; there were over seven SS men, and the crew of the Tiger were easily outgunned. Reluctantly, Otto engaged the gears and Greim shut the hatch, as the four continued onwards to join the ill-fated defence. Otto felt rather disconnected, seeing the streets he had so often visited as a child broken by war. Bustling crowds replaced by sandbags. Shop fronts replaced by machine gun nests and bomb craters. It all seemed so surreal.

As they rounded the next corner, however, now continuing towards the Brandenburg gate, they soon saw the famed Reichstag. Or, as Otto saw, the skeleton of what had once been the Reichstag. For what now stood before them was a shadow of its former glory. A burnt-out shell. Several Germans, both Wehrmacht and SS, were preparing fortifications both in and around the structure, in anticipation of the Soviet arrival. At the current rate of attrition, it could only be days at most before they reached the building. The destroyed hollow stood as a fitting metaphor to the Reich's military situation, thought Otto; still nominally existent, but any former strength or glory had long disappeared.

Finally, after a few more minutes meandering through barricades and defences in Tiergarten, the crew sighted the opera house in which resided Herr Krukenberg and his staff officers, attempting to direct the battle happening at Hermannplatz. Overshadowed by the tremendous bullet-riddled Brandenburg gate, the officers plotted to remedy the situation, as if they deluded themselves to be Frederick the Great. The crew dismounted their machine and hurried inside, hoping for a small reprieve in shell fire that would allow them to cross safely. Krukenberg stood at a wide table, with a number of individuals moving troops on a map. Various runners approached the table to convey news or orders, only to be sent away with a dismissive wave of the hand. What struck Otto as odd, however, was that when a shell exploded nearby, all around Krukenberg ducked, attempting to avoid any shrapnel, while he seemed unbothered, so resigned to his fate was he that any attempt to save himself seemed futile.

He was speaking a mixture of French and German to his subordinates. Herr Krukenberg was, Otto remembered, head of SS Sturmbattalion 'Charlemagne', the French SS volunteers, and seemed to have been made head of the SS Panzergrenadier Division 'Nordland' also, encompassing an array of German, Danish and Norwegian personnel. Otto could not understand why such a melting pot of foreign volunteers wished to commit themselves to the doomed defence of Berlin, until he realised that this was all they had left. When the Reich fell, the SS would have to go down with it, so mired was it in atrocities. Quite as their insignia suggested; victory, or death. Greim approached the table first.

"Reporting for duty, Herr Brigadeführer. Fully armed Tiger with crew," he said.

Technically the Tiger was fully armed, but with the miniscule number of shells available for its main gun it was almost a lie. Krukenberg, however, seemed relieved at another heavy tank to reinforce his men.

"I am glad to see you, damn it," he sighed, rubbing his brow. "We tried to conduct a counterattack near Treptow park with our remaining Tigers. After that was mauled, we tried again with assault guns, failing again. I've ordered a withdrawal to Hermannplatz, but that won't hold for long. We have a machine gun nest currently holding Halensee bridge; I want you to go to Neukölln and help the rearguard evacuate wounded, then get back here," he ordered.

Otto struggled to make his mind up about Krukenberg; he

seemed to have a concern for his troops, yet was this simple pragmatism? He was the leader of the Charlemagne battalion, made of former French collaborators, and doubtless responsible for innumerable atrocities. Otto simply chose not to think about it, mostly due to the complex nature of the situation rather than the usual simplicity of ignoring what went on.

The team climbed aboard their weary war wagon and proceeded onwards to Neukölln. They were, each crew member knew, heading towards an unforgiving battle. They would be largely unsupported by fellow armour and would be up against an overwhelming enemy. Even the most cocksure of fighters would recognise that the situation was unlikely to lead to success. Yet, they continued. For the wounded, if no one else. Otto had seen far too many innocents pressed into the service of evil, or sane made to serve the insane. Alexei, for one, a young man with the world at his feet, his life snatched over a measly cottage in an already won war. His letter continued to warm Otto's pocket, urging to be delivered. Did his love even know? Did she still think he was serving the motherland just as the crew's relations felt they served the fatherland? Had he even been found, or was he simply rotting in the ditch Otto had killed and left him in?

Through his periscope Otto started to witness the sights of active battle. He saw soldiers limping in the direction from whence the Tiger had come, sometimes carried by their comrades. He saw field medics applying bandages to motionless wounded, injecting morphine and stabilising injuries. Young boys of the Hitler youth cowered behind rubble, shell-shocked and horrified at the bloodshed. The occasional bullet zipped across the concrete, as they neared the rifle and machine gun fire. Neukölln town hall seemed the forward headquarters of the division, with officers evidently preparing to evacuate.

The crew got to work right away. They pulled the Tiger up alongside an improvised medical station, manned by one doctor and one assistant to perhaps forty casualties.

"Gather all wounded with a chance of survival," ordered Greim. His face was intensely sombre, with the grave knowledge that his valued comrades would be forced to play God, deciding life or death for the wounded. Otto flung open his hatch, MP40 swung behind him, and climbed into the hell which surrounded them. The stench was unbearable. Death, blood, smoke. Otto had to stop a moment, trying to steel himself against fainting when confronted with such destruction. He jumped from the tank, his boots crunching on the rubble and broken glass underfoot and made his way towards the row of wounded men. Kellerman joined him, while Greim and Scholl remained in the Tiger to operate the gun.

The pair walked towards the doctor. He was sawing an arm from an unconscious man on the table, while his assistant did the best to stem the blood flow. When Kellerman attempted to speak with the doctor, he simply barked for them to wait, and continued the surgery. After a few moments, he removed the arm from the operating table, and turned to the crew members.

"What do you want?" he asked. His manner was sharp, devoid of patience, though with the amount of work surrounding him Otto could hardly hold it against the doctor. Frankly if he had slapped the two with the severed arm it would have been understandable. Otto informed them of their mission, and he appeared relieved to have some of his casualties evacuated to the rear, if only to give him more time for each patient.

And with that, they set to work. Otto searched the rows for those visibly eligible for triage, the conscious or those with stabilised bleeds. He helped a few of the lesser harmed individuals climb aboard the Tiger, while the doctor's assistant helped him lift those unable to stand. Kellerman and the doctor himself also worked at loading the Tiger with wounded, the vast majority sitting on top of the hull and turret. As Otto knelt to lift another wounded man, another person grabbed him. Turning, Otto saw a boy, sixteen years old at most, clawing at his ankle.

"Am I going to die?" he asked Otto, his voice quivering and eyes teared. Unsure what to say, Otto simply held the young man's hand.

"Of course you won't," he replied, attempting to keep his voice soothing amidst his own fear for the boy's chances. He patted the boy's hand and stood up; the youth's other hand was desperately trying to hold in his intestines, and it was clear to see that he was not long for the world. Otto's reassurance stood as a mere white lie, to ease his passing into eternity.

The Tiger was now covered in wounded soldiers, and it was time for the crew to mount up and retreat to Krukenberg's headquarters. Kellerman had got back inside, while Otto and the assistant wrenched the last of the casualties aboard.

"Thank you for your help," Otto told the assistant with a half-smile.

The assistant replied, sighing with exhaustion, "We do what we can, but—"

Warm blood spattered across Otto's face. The crack of a

rifle shot could be heard, before machine gun fire erupted again, much closer this time than it had been before. The assistant's face was one of shock and fear, staring wildly into Otto's eyes, into his soul, before he collapsed onto the floor. Blood pulsated from his throat, flowing down his medical overalls at an alarming rate; a bullet had caught the side of his neck, piercing the artery. Otto dropped to put pressure on the wound, while the assistant grasped at him. He could feel the pulse in his hands as he tried to stop the blood escape through his fingers.

The Tiger fired a deafening shot in the direction of a rubble barricade ahead of the street, striking one of two T-34s which had emerged over its brow. This was clearly a renewed Soviet assault, and the MG34 and MG42 nests began to open a hail of fire in an attempt to contain the Red Army assault battalions which were clearing the houses each side of the street. The second T-34 was turning its gun to face the Tiger, but before it had completed its rotation, two Panzerfaust warheads slammed into its side. The smoke trails showed that the shots had been from a cellar; a Soviet flamethrower team ran to the opening and filled it with fire. Grenades were also hurled into the inferno, and a squad kicked in the door of the building. Otto was still with the assistant, who was spluttering blood and growing weaker by the second.

"We need to go, Griff, now!" yelled Greim, attempting to keep his head low in the gunfire. Otto stood from the assistant, who looked at him with such fear. 'Don't leave me,' he might have said, if he could have done. But instead he stared, afraid, until Otto tore himself away from the dying man and jumped into his driver's seat. Another T-34 was crippled by Panzerfaust operators, two tall SS men who managed to retreat successfully after firing. Otto began to reverse the Tiger, machine guns engaging the Soviet hoard. Several shots pinged from the hull, some finding the bodies of the wounded stowed on the armour, who fell off of the Panzer. "Faster!" yelled Greim. "Get back to Hermannplatz!"

Otto reversed the crew left, in order to break the line of sight from the assault. The number of Soviet troops surely amounted to a full breakthrough, and Otto was curious as to where the division would next be posted. They were passed by a Tiger II, the newer iteration of their own machine, rolling towards the combat. They had noticed a number of these knocked out in the streets, yet this was the first time in a while that they had seen one working. It was a mighty beast, but cumbersome, and ate fuel at an extraordinary rate. Their own Tiger, however, decorated with the dead and dying, continued to move towards Krukenberg's headquarters.

When they arrived, they saw that the whole opera house was being evacuated. The wounded were quickly taken from the top of the Tiger by soldiers, and the crew went inside the building in search of their commander. There were only a handful of officers and troops, however, gathering maps and documents.

"Brigadeführer Krukenberg is setting up the new headquarters, at the Stadtmitte U-Bahn station. Go there now," reported one of the officers, as the building continued to shake with the explosion of nearby shells.

The withdrawal to an underground station would prevent the armour from defending the group, and so it remained a mystery to Otto as to where they would be deployed. They pulled up near the underground station entrance, and descended the stairs, with Otto and Scholl carrying one of the remaining casualties that the Tiger had ferried from the front. The man was wounded, but not critically so; a piece of shrapnel had prevented him placing weight upon his leg, but the bleeding had been controlled. He was an older Volkssturm man, tired of the fighting, having likely seen action in the previous war.

As they reached the underground citadel, it was like another world. Officers were awarding medals to young boys. Old men sat bleeding on the tracks. Several soldiers scoffed the scraps of food they had found in the momentary break they had, understanding that it may be the last chance they had to eat. Greim continued into the rail carriage, which was being used as Krukenberg's headquarters, while the rest of the crew sat with a group of Wehrmacht veterans eating round a fire. One of the men handed Otto a small tin of gruel with a faint smile, for which he thanked them.

"So where are you lot from then?" asked the stranger, eating his food. Otto tasted the disgustingly thin gruel, but knew he needed the energy.

"We got cut off from the ninth," replied Otto, adding, "We have been fighting a long road to get back to Berlin." The soldier chuckled.

"What a waste of time that was," he laughed.

The crew half laughed and continued to eat. Otto, however, lay back, and attempted to catch perhaps ten minutes of sleep. It was difficult, of course, amongst the screams, smells, sounds of men readying themselves for battle, and the flickering of the lights as artillery and bombs continued to crash down overhead. But he managed, and lay amongst the chaos; he would probably never sleep again.

Chapter 11
Stadtmitte U-Bahn Station

A particularly ferocious explosion overhead shook Otto from his snatched slumber. He sat up steadily, trying to regain his bearings; to wake in such pandemonium was rather unnerving. Scholl and Kellerman still sat with him, swapping stories with the exhausted Wehrmacht personnel gathered around the modest fire. Greim had not yet re-emerged from the U-Bahn carriage, which was crowded with various officers and runners attempting to coordinate the battle raging above ground. It was difficult for Otto to get much of an idea what was going on, but the odd snippet of conversation he was able to overhear painted a grim picture. The fortifications around Hermannplatz had been completely breached, and the Nordland division was facing a full withdrawal into the central district if they failed to counterattack.

    A contingent of SS and Hitler Youth soldiers entered the station, wide smiles on their faces. They revealed themselves to be French volunteers, fighting under the SS Charlemagne battalion, Krukenberg's former command, and boasted in mixed French and German of their victories over enemy tanks. Apparently, they had accrued upwards of ten Soviet armour kills, with the help of the Hitler Youth and Panzerfausts. This was an impressive haul, no doubt, yet it remained futile in the face of the Russian tide; knock out as many enemy tanks as the soldiers might, and there remained ten to replace each one. Such kills would only delay the inevitable.

Soon after, Greim emerged from the makeshift command carriage, his face sombre. He trudged dejectedly towards the crew, preparing to issue the orders he had been given. No man expected the orders he would give to be easy.

"We are to counterattack," he sighed.

"Coordinate with the remaining armour in order to provide a rear-guard action. This will allow some of the Nordland units which have been cut off to retreat into the central district. Following their evacuation Westwards, we take up positions in the Tiergarten, to hold off the enemy armour."

"For what, an hour at most?" questioned Kellerman, palpable sarcasm in his voice.

"To follow our orders, Kellerman. Now let's get to it," responded Greim, sharply. It was clear he was as sceptical about the orders as any of them, but harsh military discipline seemed the only way to maintain order in this mess.

The crew stood, and bid their farewells to the Wehrmacht soldiers, wishing them luck, and that they might get out of the city. They climbed the steps and emerged into the urban hell once more. The droning hum of unchallenged Russian aircraft sounded overhead, with whatever remained of the Luftwaffe nowhere to be seen. Some streets had been cleared, according to the soldiers Otto had been speaking with, in order to create makeshift runways for German fighters, although the sheer difference in numbers between the air forces would render them relatively useless. The crew remounted their Tiger, alongside what remained of the Panzergrenadier division's armoured column. There survived a handful of King Tigers,

Tiger Is, Sturmgeschütze (or 'Stug' for short), and the odd Panzer IV. It would be difficult to cooperate with the other tanks due to the Tiger's defunct radio, though by the look of their comrade's machines no one seemed in a good state of repair.

The column moved off, the collective revving of the engines providing some company to the so often lonely sound of the crew's own machine. The crew's vehicle was around halfway along the row of roughly twelve machines. Otto simply tried to maintain the distance between himself and the tank ahead of him, as artillery continued to crash around them, and the contingent wound through the desolate ruin of a city. The sound of gunfire was again growing louder, as they neared the front; Greim's hatch was open, and he was talking with the various tank commanders, warning them to watch the corners. Just as the lead Tiger II's commander turned to check what advice was being passed up the line, however, a shell slammed into the side of his tank, and he fell back into the now flaming turret. The shot had ripped through the engine block, proceeded by the tell-tale whistle of a high velocity round.

As the destroyed tank's crew attempted to escape the fiery hull, the other vehicles wheeled right to face the aggressor, and took up a combat spread formation. Greim shut his hatch, and yelled to the crew.

"Be ready to engage enemy armour, and maintain spacing from our allies! Don't get bunched up!"

Otto, his heart pounding in his ears as he prepared for the fury of fighting, turned their machine to the right, and scanning the street for enemy positions. A KV-2 heavy tank seemed to have been responsible for the first shot, but Scholl swiftly landed a well-placed shot into the Soviet vehicle's hull, which subsequently stopped moving. The Panzer IV just behind them fired an accompanying shell, striking the turret and causing the enemy to erupt in a golden ball as the ammunition rack exploded, and the turret to be launched skywards.

The German unit continued forwards, machine guns doing their best to pin the Soviet positions on the street ahead. There were, for now, no other Russian tanks in view, and so the German armour continued relatively unchallenged. Scholl rotated the turret back and forth, checking for enemies, while Greim tried to work out the best way to go.

"Most of the remaining troops are still held up in and around the opera house, cut off in the retreat. If we can get there and provide some cover, even for a few minutes, the troops will be able to reinforce Krukenberg's defences. Take point, Griff," he ordered.

Otto moved their Tiger to the front of the column, while Greim reopened his hatch and gestured the other tanks to follow.

They were a street block or two from the former headquarters but were only able to move steadily in order to adequately check for Russian tank hunters. They moved into a narrow street, only just wide enough to accommodate the accompanying King Tigers. With the Tiger's gun fixed ahead, Otto continued to slowly open the throttle; while they needed to be careful in such an area, it was important to get back into more manoeuvrable wide roads as soon as possible, to avoid being trapped. His thinking was soon vindicated; a number of captured Panzerfausts fired from one of the street cellars, sending plumes of smoke as they penetrated the armour of the Panzer IV, perhaps four vehicles behind their own Tiger. The Panzer rattled to a halt, crashing into the wall with thick black smoke emerging from the engine. Judging by the number of successful hits dealt to the machine, all of its crew were likely dead or injured. One of the Stugs towards the rear of the column landed a shot instantaneously into the cellar from whence the shots had originated, causing dust to erupt from the orifice. The crew of the Tiger II behind the destroyed Panzer dismounted their tank and hurled grenades into the cellar, to ensure the threat was neutralised.

As some of the other tank's crew searched the Panzer IV for survivors, and carefully pulled the injured loader from the turret amidst screams of pains, the commander approached their own Tiger. Otto, Scholl and Kellerman kept their gaze firmly fixed upon the end of the street; if the Soviets chose to attack now and disabled their Tiger, a large portion of German armour would be caught between the two knocked out tanks, stuck as sitting ducks.

"You four will need to carry on without us, we are blocked by the destroyed Panzer," called up the King Tiger commander to Greim. "We will try to find a way around, and meet you at the opera house if we can. If we are unable to proceed, we will retreat to Tiergarten and hopefully await your return."

"If we are to bear the brunt of the advance, could you cough up any spare shells? Perhaps from one of the other Tiger Is?" replied Greim, frustrated at their newly lacking support.

The other commander went to scavenge ammunition along the line, while Greim briefed the crew. "Right, there are only four of us now. We have two Stugs and a King Tiger, and so are going to be limited for movement speed. Don't take any risks; Griff, if it gets too hot, then pull us away. If our entire armoured section is lost, it will leave the other detachment critically under reinforced at Tiergarten. We get to the opera house, we do what we can, and we leave, no heroics," he ordered. The crew all nodded the affirmative, and soon the commander returned with a hessian sack of shells.

"Five is all I can give you, I'm afraid. Good luck lads, I hope to see you again!" he exclaimed. And with that, Otto engaged the forward gear, and carried their small cadre of machines onwards.

The squad of tanks poured out into the open street, carefully checking each direction as they emerged. Otto could see no hostile threat through his periscope, with Scholl also searching for enemies. Greim instructed him to pull left, and Otto obliged, trying to keep the Tiger close to potential cover and away from the centre of the street wherever possible. Judging by the proximity of raging battle they could not be far from the opera house, where the Soviet assault was attempting to clear up the rest of the Nordland division before moving further into the city – and winning, by the sound of it. Greim opened his hatch and gestured for the column to make the next turn right, which would be the last junction before they arrived at the former headquarters. They were frightfully under-armed to counterattack a Soviet force, and so would only be able to provide temporary cover to retreaters.

Cautiously, Otto rounded the next corner. He could see the opera house, in the square which the street led into. It was riddled with bullet holes, small fires, smoke, and shells. German soldiers continued to fiercely defend from the windows, taking pot shots at the Russian attackers, until they were suppressed by bursts of enemy rifle and machine gun fire. There remained a small number of Flak 88 anti-aircraft hybrid guns, being used in their anti-tank role, which were firing on Russian tanks as they approached the small perimeter, alongside machine gun nests. As they neared the house, Otto noticed something truly horrifying; the guns were being manned by children. Small groups of Hitler Youth, perhaps the odd Volkssturm or Wehrmacht soldier dispersed between them, were struggling to load and fire the large artillery pieces. One emplacement was operated solely by members of the League of German Maidens, the Hitler Youth's female counterpart. Few Soviet tanks had yet challenged the stronghold, though many were sure to arrive shortly, and annihilate the defenders. Small field guns were also being set up by attacking Russians, targeted to pound the thin defensive line.

"Speed up, Griff! We need to get the evacuation underway before the bulk of enemy armour arrives!" yelled Greim.

Despite feeling exposed by the lack of surrounding infantry support, Otto obeyed the command, and opened the throttle to carry the Tiger into a sprint, ready to hunt once more. The turret mounted machine gun was already opening up suppressive fire on Soviet assault groups, which were flooding forth from the other streets adjoined to the square. The plentiful rubble which scattered the streets was a haven for the Russian shock troops, who were able to approach the defensive line with relative ease. The small group of German tanks began to open fire, with Scholl targeting the larger gatherings of enemy troops, unleashing the Tiger's roaring cannon.

As they reached the end of the street, and opened into the square, Otto became fully struck by the overwhelming odds which faced them. Of around five roads branching from the plaza, only the one through which they had travelled was free from hostiles. Russian troops were approaching from nearly all directions, setting up guns in the streets and clearing rubble for their tanks to approach. The defenders were burning ammunition at a worrying rate in their attempt to hold off the Soviet personnel, while medics rushed around to treat those injured by increasingly accurate Russian fire. Shots began to strike and ricochet from the Tiger's hull, filling the cabin with the sound of pinging bullets which Otto tried to keep his focus away from.

One of the field guns fired in the direction of the tanks, narrowly whizzing past one of the accompanying Stugs. Before Scholl had a chance to respond, one of the Flak 88s delivered a surprisingly accurate shell, ripping through the gun with sparks and dust thrown into the sky. It had likely been eying up the target for a long time, as the young teenagers which operated it seemed unable to believe their success. They were clearly not seasoned veterans, able to take such a shot with minimal aim checking. The German tank consignment fanned out into the square; Otto moved the Tiger alongside one of the Stugs to the right of the opera house doorway, while the Tiger II and other Stug moved to its left. This would provide a metal barrier to allow the staff and soldiers to evacuate down the clear street.

Greim, almost without warning, flung open his hatch and dived to the ground with a thud. He then ran inside the building, presumably to inform the staff officers about the evacuation. Meanwhile, Otto climbed across into Raeder's former seat in order to bring the bow gun of the Tiger into motion. The machine gun rattled in Otto's hands, with the tracer bullets helping him to keep the weapon on target; Soviet shock troops, however, were still advancing at great speed, zipping between pieces of cover. Scholl fired a shell at one of the sandbag positions which had been occupied by the advancing Russians, sending both bags and corpses across the street. There was no breaking in the firing at any point; it was some of the fiercest combat Otto had ever seen.

The young driver almost jumped out of his skin when he heard a thud at the roof. It was dull, indicating a large enough impact, more than a simple grenade or shell. It had some metallic element but had not struck with the speed of a shell or weapon, precluding a bomb or some deadly item. Could it be a Russian soldier, who had clambered aboard and was ready to kill the occupants? Or Greim, reaching the Tiger, but shot before he was able to open the hatch? The prospect of his commander killed began to grip Otto with increasing panic.

"Can you cover me, Peter? I'll check what that is!" yelled Otto, struggling to make his voice heard above the sheer volume of gunfire. Scholl nodded, not taking his eyes from his targets as he continued to fire, and so Otto opened his hatch, and prepared to hastily glance at whatever had crashed unto the Tiger's roof.

It was not Greim, nor a Russian soldier. Sprawled across the Tiger's turret was the lifeless body of an elderly man. He seems to have fallen from one of the windows of the opera house, having been shot in the chest according to his wound. His face was twisted in shock, and terror at his fall. He was probably dead before he hit the tank. The man was dressed in civilian hat and trousers, but his coat was a First World War tunic, bearing a Wilhelmine iron cross, attained in the conflict. This old man, who had fought so hard for his country in the 'War to End All Wars', had been dragged into yet another pointless conflict brought about by too many people reminding themselves not to think about it. What would this man have thought of the Germany he had been presented with in his dying moments? A once glorious Prussianised kingdom, hijacked by fanatic right wing radicals, tainted with terrible crimes, and brought to the depths of destruction. All that had been achieved in thousands of years, wiped out in a mere moment.

Tearing himself from his thoughts, Otto ducked back into the cabin and closed his hatch before he found himself in the same position as the poor Volkssturm veteran. He continued to blast the advancing Soviets, who were dashing between the available cover with tremendous bravery. Judging by the increasing number of defending casualties, and the occasional explosion, it became evident that the most advanced Russian squads had got within grenade-throwing distance of the outer line. Time was running out for what remained of the division.

A hatch on the Tiger's turret was flown open, and Otto readied his MP40, expecting an enemy arrival. Instead, Greim dropped into the cabin and shut the opening behind himself; their commander had been wounded in his shoulder, and since been bandaged, but his full range of movement suggested that the injury was not serious enough to warrant much concern.

"Are you all right, sir?" asked Kellerman, gesturing to the injured shoulder. Greim nodded exhaustedly amidst panting, and moved straight onto the next brief for his men.

"They are evacuating now; we need to give them five minutes if we can," informed Greim. "The staff officers and veterans will be prioritised, heading down the street from whence we came and reinforcing Krukenberg's line."

Otto was well aware that even five minutes would be difficult to survive in this hell, and so remained ready to switch back to the driver's position and evacuate the machine and crew at a moment's notice. The bow mounted MG34 was beginning to run short on ammunition, and if possible, Otto would prefer that he avoid loading more ammo until they were ready to move back to Tiergarten, considering the extremely limited supply situation. Time was of the essence, especially since the dreaded green silhouettes of Soviet armour were beginning to fill the streets leading to the square. T-34s, KV1s, KV2s and IS tanks were rumbling towards the opera house, winding through the debris and beginning to fling shells at the besieged building.

The Flak 88s began to come into action; though a formidable tank-hunter on paper, their effectiveness when operated by conscripted children was guaranteed to be limited. The Tiger's gun was also doing its best to hold off the enemy tanks, while remaining economic with its ammunition. One of the Flak guns managed to disable a T-34 track, blocking the street it was on. It rotated its turret towards the offending artillery piece, with the Tiger loosing a shell just before the Soviet machine annihilated the gun position. Scholl's aim was terrific; the round tore through the side of the T-34 turret, striking with sparks as it cut through the armour of the Russian tank. It grew motionless, with the crew of the turret having been killed by the shrapnel of the Tiger's bite.

Despite certain successes, it was clear to Otto and his comrades that they were losing ground. The Russian armour was getting steadily closer, and the small number of German machines would run out of ammunition long before the Russians ran out of tanks. The King Tiger of their contingent had been struck by several shells from an IS-2, and its stillness suggested that it had been taken out of commission. The high-pitched clanking of small arms against Otto's own Tiger's hull was soon joined by the ricochet and non-penetration of enemy T-34 and field gun shells; if one of these projectiles struck at the correct angle, they would slip through the armour and into the cabin with devastating effect. It was vital that they left before that happened.

Otto's urge to leave was soon compounded in a deadly threat. A small group of IS-2 tanks was proceeding down one of the streets towards the plaza, in sight of the Tiger. Remembering how difficult it had been to challenge even one of these in the previous town, Otto became extremely panicked at the sight, and turned to Greim for instruction. He was silent, first waiting for Scholl to fire before he decided the appropriate next move. Scholl did so; not only that, but the nearest Flak 88 and Stug joined the Tiger in engaging the closest of the IS tanks, to no avail.

"Retreat!" yelled Greim, as he saw with dismay the shells shrugged casually away from the enemy tank. Otto, needing no second reminder, flung the Tiger into reverse gear and began moving away from the position as quickly as possible. Some of the personnel were leaving the opera house by now, running down the street towards the city centre.

Almost without warning, a deafening orange explosion cut through the air. The Tiger jolted at the impact, and the ears of the crew were ringing as the sound reverberated through the cabin. It became apparent that an enemy shell had struck the nearest Flak 88's ammunition stockpile, incinerating the Hitler Youth operators in an instant as the explosives were set off simultaneously. There were not even the usual bodies, or pieces of bodies, which Otto saw after most explosions. There was simply a crater, and pieces of the cannon. It was like its operators had never existed, blasted from the world. The IS-2 now rotated its turret towards Otto's retreating Tiger, and prepared to deliver a killing blow.

A thunderous explosion sounded through the Tiger, but it was not their own hull which had been breached. Flames were licking up from the engine and hatches of the Russian tank, its turret still fixated on their own vehicle. The Stug had not fired, and so it remained a mystery as to what had neutralised their opponent. Suddenly, a Tiger II roared out of one of the smaller sideroads which led into the square. The other half of the armoured column! The remaining tanks of the Nordland division must have found their way through the labyrinth of debris and made it to the square; a handful of tanks rolled into the street and began firing on the Soviet armour. It could provide a few crucial moments for the battle-weary first half of the group to retreat into Tiergarten, while the rest of the Opera house personnel moved to the subterranean citadel of Krukenberg's command centre.

"Go, reverse!" yelled Greim, with a signalling kick to Otto's shoulder. Returning the tank to reverse gear, Otto moved the vehicle towards the safe street from which they had originated. Only their Tiger and accompanying Stug were left out of their original four, and the pair made for the Brandenburg gate. Otto locked one of the tracks before engaging forward gear, spinning the Tiger into the direction which they travelled. Through his periscope, Otto now saw the retreat-turned-rout being undertaken by the Nordland division. The wounded were being carried between fellow comrades, or dragged in some of the worst cases. Volkssturm were discarding their weapons and running for the alleyways in the street, the slower and older of them being gunned down by zealous officers determined to win the unwinnable. The street lights were morbidly decorated with the dead; supposed 'traitors to the Reich', hanged for imagined offences and the reasonable wish to retreat. It was cruelly ironic, the regime which had betrayed the German people was so fervently punishing others for supposed transgressions.

Shells continued to rack the road, shrapnel often finding a home in the bodies of the retreating soldiers. Berlin had been one of the most fervent of opponents to the Nazis during the last free Weimar elections, yet now the city bled in one of the most brutal battles of the war. Gallows humour had turned to reality, fears realised, families burned and separated, men killed, women raped, and children orphaned. It seemed to be truly the end of days, not just for Berliners, but for a human race which was able to call such destruction upon one another.

Otto wound their machine through a small snicket of a side street, in order to break the line of sight between the Tiger and the Russian tanks which were sure to begin their pursuit shortly. Between the piles of rubble, the Brandenburg gate was clearly visible, towering over the ruins. That was their heading; beyond the gate they would find the Tiergarten, in which they would take up defensive positions. To what end, no one was exactly sure. But for now, they had a purpose, and set about to achieve it as best they could. The fuel remaining in the Tiger's tank was beginning to run thin, but would be sufficient to take them to their next posting; it was unlikely that they would need to move any further.

Bricks and pieces of concrete crackled under the rattling tracks as the tank rolled forwards, spotting the odd straggler limping through the buildings. Distant gunfire was spitting up again, closer this time, near the Stadtmitte station, Krukenberg's headquarters. Otto could see the end of the street through his periscope, which led onto the wider thoroughfare down which they needed to travel. Greim gestured Scholl to direct his aim left, to scan for targets when the Tiger emerged, and Kellerman held a spare shell at the ready. Cautiously, Otto allowed the hull of the Tiger to stick out into the street, perhaps a few feet, to check for hostile activity. Receiving no incoming fire, he edged the rest of the vehicle forwards until it was in full view. The road was quiet, bewitched by a deadly silence. The drumfire across the city continued, but there were no signs of activity in this snicket. The Russian assault was busy finishing off the remnants of resistance in the city's Eastern sectors, a brief reprieve before they smashed through the next line of futile defence.

Passing under the great Brandenburg gate, the Tiger finally arrived in the Tiergarten, and began searching for a position among the trees. Otto realised that their accompanying Stug had gone missing, failing to follow them through the side road, and was curious as to its current position.

"Herr Hauptman, where is our Stug support? Will they meet us in Tiergarten?" he asked Greim, hoping that he would have the answer.

"For now, Griff, assume that we are the last piece of armour in Berlin. That way, anyone else we find will be a nice surprise."

The crew found it in themselves to laugh, while at the same time wondering if Greim's prediction was in fact true.

Otto found a place for the Tiger to take refuge, near the main path, where they would be able to see units approaching while they themselves remained hidden until the enemy was very close. Greim nodded, approving the defensive position.

For a likely final resting place, the crew seemed to agree upon it with almost no thought or discussion, acknowledging the lack of any taxable situation in which they might last more than a few hours. It was slightly away from the main thoroughfare of the Tiergarten, leading from the Brandenburg gate, and perhaps five metres into the trees. It was indeed visible from the road, if slightly camouflaged, and could be fired on by enemy armour. It was a paltry defence.

Once he had reversed into position, allowing the turret the widest possible arc of fire through the foliage, Otto turned to Greim and awaited further instructions. The commander stopped a moment, surveying the area through his now opened hatch, and weighing his options.

"Set up a machine gun nest with the high mounted MG42. Otto and Scholl, you will man it, and try to pin the enemy infantry while Kellerman and I take out the hostile armour," he ordered. "If you are quick about it you should be able to steal some sandbags from the nearby buildings or from around the park, which should provide you some protection." Greim's orders might have sounded like an action plan, but his tone made painfully clear that even their militaristic commander had little hope for their ever escaping alive. Otto and Scholl dismounted their tank without a word, and began trudging towards the Brandenburg gate once more, in search of cover.

"You know, I always wanted to see Berlin," said Scholl, gazing at the Brandenburg gate. He laughed and pushed Otto's shoulder, continuing, "I wasn't expecting it to be quite so… smoke covered, I must say," he chortled.

It was true, the capital seemed in an especially sorry state for any would-be tourist seeing it for the first time. Otto had grown up not far from the city, and so he had seen it in its former glory many times before; he couldn't decide, however, if this made it easier or worse to see the settlement wrapped in such destruction. It was beyond recognition; if it weren't for landmarks such as the gate or the Reichstag, Otto would almost have thought he was in one of the cities deep into the Eastern front, one already taken and retaken a number of times, evacuated and bombed, deconstructed into rubble. Berlin fit some of these criteria, except in a few crucial ways. This was still the capital of the Reich. And, perhaps more significantly, it hadn't been evacuated. The city still lived, still breathed, with a suffering and mauled population trapped within.

They arrived at the Brandenburg gate, and began searching for defence. The windows had not been reinforced, and defensive lines not yet established, while most of the fighting continued in other areas. This was a brief calm before the storm. Straggling Wehrmacht and Volkssturm members could be seen pouring into the Tiergarten, some as individuals or small groups, and some as organised formations. They began setting up snipers, Panzerfaust operators, and riflemen along the roads and in the buildings to hold the advance for some time. Finally, Otto and Scholl found some sandbags in a small Anti-Aircraft site which had been hit by a bomb, destroying the occupants and equipment. One operator lay dead a few metres away, thrown by the blast, while his comrades had been all but eviscerated. Otto and Scholl picked up some of the intact bags, while some of the retreating soldiers helped them in carrying the bags. Otto picked up the last bag, having first to brush a severed ear of one of the operators from the canvas, and followed Scholl back towards the Tiger.

The pair stacked the bags in a low semicircle connected to the Tiger's hull, on its left side, away from the path. Greim handed them the machine gun from the tank, stowed and mountable on the roof. They balanced it in a vee shape in the sandbags, aimed towards the Brandenburg gate, and audited their supplies. Two boxes of MG42 ammunition, three MP40 magazines, and a handful of grenades. This would not last long, and they both knew it.

"Herr Hauptman, we have almost no ammunition, what should we do?" asked Scholl, shrugging with confusion. Pausing for a moment, Greim instructed them to ask the Wehrmacht personnel if any of them had spare munitions, or otherwise to scavenge from the buildings. Scholl set off for some of the Nordland troops which were digging foxholes around the path, while Otto stripped down the machine gun and cleaned its components.

Kellerman emerged from the vehicle to light his pipe, and called down to Otto. "Do you even know how to use that thing, Griff? A little heavy for you, no?" he jeered.

Otto returned his laughter, replying, "If I can handle the Tiger, then I don't imagine this will be too much!"

Greim was cleaning his rifle, ready to use as a last resort should all the shells be used up. Despite the hopelessness of the situation, his strict military demeanour was unshaken; Greim knew that he would need to stay strong for his troops, in order to set the necessary example. Any sane man would have run from Berlin as quickly as his legs would carry him, and it was the task of the commander to help them forget the ludicrous nature of their task.

Otto reassembled, loaded, and cocked the weapon, and glanced upwards just as Scholl approached. He was carrying two cans of MG42 ammunition, and a Kar98k rifle.

"A group over there sacrificed a few belts of ammo, on the condition that I swapped my MP40 for one of their rifles; gives them more firepower, they said."

The machine gun was going to be more important in the upcoming engagement, and so any sacrifice to keep the weapon firing was more than worthwhile. Soon after, a few remnants of the armoured column which had survived the engagement at the opera house rolled along the gravel path, crackling as the tracks spun and buried the vehicles into defence positions.

Before Otto had time to count the number of allied tanks remaining, or inform Greim of their approach, a distant whooshing sound signalled the approach of enemy artillery fire. The deep booming of Russian guns heralded a barrage in preparation for the next attack. The Soviet tide was coming to drown them.

Greim heard the fire, and yelled to his crew, "Get aboard the tank, the rain is coming!"

Otto and Scholl dived back into their positions, discarding the weapons and ammunition in the sandbag circle and hoping that they wouldn't receive a direct hit. Closing the hatch with a creek, and feeling the cold metal lid shut above him, Otto sat low in his seat, and prayed for the shells to miss them. Artillery fell all around the Panzer, with dirt pattering across the hull, and the occasional pieces of shrapnel striking the armour. It would not be long before the swarms of enemy soldiers, filled with vengeance, would be upon them.

Chapter 12
Tiergarten, Berlin

The crew of the Tiger were silent, while shellfire continued to rack the ground around them. No man dared speak, but instead made their peace with what would happen to them. Otto thumbed the rough paper of Alexei's letter, still housed in his tunic pocket, and regretted that he would likely never manage to pass it to the intended recipient. He took it out and glanced once more at its contents, the ill lit cabin narrowly illuminating the scrawled Russian words, while the bottom corner was spattered in a patch of browned dry blood. The quality of the writing was rather poor, indicating that Alexei likely wrote the letter in strained times, perhaps while on the march. These words for a lover sat in Otto's hand, locked in Cyrillic code unbreakable to Otto.

Kellerman broke the silence of the solemn crew by asking the one question which everyone thought, but no one dared air.

"Why are we carrying this on, Herr Hauptmann?" he sighed. "The war is lost, why don't we hand ourselves over? Or stage an escape of the city?"

Such defeatism, which might have been punished or reprimanded at earlier stages of the war, now went totally unaddressed, simply proven by its insurmountable evidence. Greim took a moment to consider his answer before speaking.

"You know, before I was reassigned here, back in 1941 I

was part of the first wave in Operation Barbarossa. We still rode high on our glorious victories of the previous summer in France. Damned if we didn't feel quite invincible, you know. Punching through Red army divisions as if they existed in name only. 'Righteous wind', that was the name of my Panzer IV. Ironic, considering what we did with it." Greim's usual stern demeanour was broken for a moment, as his eyes glazed over with nostalgia.

"We hit Minsk; I was in army group centre. My God, the destruction. The fires, they still light up my dreams. We had brought forth hell, and unleashed it on earth. Shattered homes, disabled wrecks of tanks, swathes of corpses, and fleeing soldiers. I truly believed, back then. Not in the purported 'racial superiority' that those bile coughers back at the propaganda ministry would tell you, but in the indestructibility of the German soldier. The moral incorruptibility. But the things that I saw, the things that we did..." His voice tailed off, as he tried to gather his thoughts, and articulate his memories. Otto, Kellerman and Scholl had served with Stoltz, their previous commander, in Greece, and then North Africa, and so had been spared the horrors of the Eastern front for some time. They were reassigned to Italy, and only went to the East in the latter half of 1944, and had therefore fought a quite different war to that of Greim.

"Prisoners," he continued, "would be lucky not to be shot on sight. If they survived briefly, they were taken to POW or concentration camps. Those places, there was no food, no humanity. They were holes to die in. And the cruelty wasn't restricted to Soviet soldiers, but women and children too. Men too old for the draft, Jews, Roma, anyone considered inferior. Every time I close my eyes, I see it. The SS, even Wehrmacht and local auxiliaries. All participants in this orgy of violence. That is why we can't surrender. We are too far gone; we are beyond salvation. They will never forgive what we have done, and I should expect a quicker death if we simply fight on. Germany is going down in flames, and I intend to go with her, if only to forget what I have seen."

Otto was almost moved to tears, as the fact he had known for so long dawned into his consciousness. This was it. They were going to die. There were no more orders, no more tangible objectives to obtain. The crew were quiet, stunned into silence at their commander's emotional revelation. The peace, however, revealed that the shellfire had now ceased. They now entered the golden handful of seconds before the Soviet assault commenced. Otto grasped the handle of his escape hatch and flung it open. The metal was cold, lifeless. The sky revealed above was choked with smoke and destruction, with the sound of battle was emerging once more. Explosions, rifle fire, machine gun bursts, grenades, artillery, tanks, aircraft, all filling the air with the devil's orchestra.

Otto's boots crunched on the soil and stones which had been flung over the Tiger's hull, as he stepped down to man his machine gun. Scholl joined him, working the bolt action of his rifle, and the two men prepared to defend their tank. The soil beneath them was soft, spongy. Otto cocked the weapon, and fixed his eyes on the sights, peering through the burned-out trees. While some retained their leaves, many had been damaged or destroyed in the shelling, not to mention previous bombs having fallen on the area by the allies. British Lancasters had regularly raided the city, bringing a prelude of devastation before the defence of the city had started.

Looking around, he could see that a small number of tanks

had joined them from the Nordland armoured column. A mixture of SS and Wehrmacht vehicles, a few King Tigers and a Stug had arrived safely alongside their own machine, but it was a paltry handful. They would not survive for long, but were better than nothing. Wehrmacht troops were screaming nearby, injured in the shelling, while medics buzzed around performing triage or dragging the wounded to safety. Severed limbs, shattered skulls, and entrails cruelly decorated the park, in a gory mayday fair. But there was little time to observe such horrific surroundings, as the noise of battle drew steadily closer, and Russian troops crossed through the Brandenburg gate.

The ground shook with the rumble of enemy armour, while Otto waited for the infantry to draw within firing distance. His breath had frozen, and heart stopped; he felt almost as if he might faint. It was important that the crew waited until the Soviets had drawn closer, in order to maximise the effect of their limited ammunition. Scholl had begun to weep beside Otto, his joviality unable to survive the impossibility of their task. Suddenly, machine gun fire ripped through the air to Otto's right, and in an instant the leading Soviet scouts were cut to pieces. One of the other remaining German tanks had opened fire prematurely, throwing all of the Russian forces into a state of high alert, and forcing Scholl and Otto to join the engagement early. Otto aimed carefully, and released short bursts from his MG42; the enemy was still too far away from their position to deliver sustained fire. The weapon jolted violently into Otto's shoulder with each pull of the trigger, the sights kicking furiously in every direction as the young driver struggled to force the barrel into line. Scholl had also started to deliver a steady patter of rifle fire, the clacking of the bolt action sounding rapidly as he cycled his rounds.

A ground-shaking boom erupted from next to the pair, as the Tiger's mighty cannon joined the fight, striking one of the enemy T-34s with its first shell. The green tank halted in its tracks and sat motionless, as thick black smoke curled from its hatches. Flames began to spurt upwards out of one opening as a Soviet tanker, himself engulfed in fire, flung himself from the cabin, writhing in pain on the ashen ground until he grew deathly still. Otto paused his fire, shaken by the horrific display, until Scholl jolted his shoulder to continue. Tracer rounds spat from the machine gun barrel, coursing through the air towards the countless advancing infantry, accompanied by the tell-tale buzz of the MG42. The Soviets were growing ever nearer their Tiger, with squads armed with PPSH41 submachine guns using shell craters left by the artillery bombardment as cover. Soon, despite his conservative use of his ammunition, Otto's weapon clicked empty, and needed reloading.

"I need a new ammunition box!" cried Otto, yelling into Scholl's ear as he struggled to be heard above the fury of combat.

Scholl prepared to switch out the overheated barrel of the weapon with a spare, while Otto fumbled with a new ammunition belt, as the enemy advanced closer. The rapidity with which he had been forced to fire the weapon meant that the barrel was growing steadily superheated, and would melt or buckle if not changed often enough. However, the usual heat resistant glove for switching it could not be found, and so Scholl paused for a moment in preparation, and proceeded to wrench the red-hot barrel from the gun with his bare hands. He cried in pain, and his hand blistered instantly with the severity of the burn, yet he continued to discard the barrel onto the floor and load its replacement. Otto prepared the ammunition required, and the weapon was ready for operation once more.

And it was not before time. A Soviet soldier leapt over their sandbag barricade, just as the pair prepared to reopen fire, armed only with a hand axe. His SMG hung loosely at his side, with magazine missing, suggesting that he had run out of ammunition. He swung his blade at Scholl, who narrowly ducked under the assault and, in a moment of incredibly quick thinking and self-sacrifice, once again picked up the searing hot spare barrel of the MG42 and lashed out at the attacker. The Russian was struck just under his eye, causing steam to arise from the dreadful burn. Screaming and clutching at his wound, the Soviet stumbled backwards, allowing Scholl enough time to grab his Kar98K and deliver a killing shot to the hostile's chest. The soldier collapsed quickly, and lay completely motionless as blood pumped lazily from the gaping wound in his chest.

Scholl was now badly burned, and struggled to continue operating the bolt action of his rifle. He carried on nevertheless, however, and Otto could tell by his bloodied hands that his skin was perishing. As for himself, Otto continued to pour fire onto the advancing enemy squads. One of the remaining Panzers, a King Tiger positioned a few metres ahead of the crew's own tank, had been overrun. Molotov cocktails and knives were being used with ferocious speed to clear out the entrenched defenders, escorted by the usual terrible screams and petrified faces. The crew's own Tiger was still spitting lead in an effort to suppress the fire from Soviets operating captured Panzerfausts, with its main armament sure to be running low on shells by now.

A horrific smashing sound made it clear to Otto that their Tiger had been struck. He turned to see the pale smoke trail of a fired Panzerfaust, which had struck the side of the Tiger. Having impacted the armour at a perpendicular angle, it had managed to partially penetrate the hull, with the soldier responsible having been gunned down immediately after he fired the weapon. Scholl and Otto exchanged glances briefly, terrified that their commander and comrade had both perished in that instant.

"You go and check; I will keep them suppressed as best as I am able. My burnt hands will be useless for applying bandages," cried Scholl, taking over the MG42 and throwing bullets across the Soviet positions. Occasional bullets were thumping into the sandbags around them, as Otto dived to the ground. He would be forced to scramble under the tank and access the emergency escape hatch, lest he be picked off when trying to open the rooftop hatches.

Otto hauled himself into the Tiger, trying to assess the situation in the dim lighting. There was a small hole in the side of the Tiger, where the projectile had pierced the hull, providing a narrow stream of light. Greim could be heard coughing, disorientated by the attack but yelling that he was unhurt. Kellerman, however, was silent. Otto climbed through the tank, until he came across his dear friend. Kellerman was hunched over in his loader's seat, and Otto reached across to wake him. Had Kellerman not heard his yelling for him? It seemed impossible for Otto that he would be deceased, so long had they served side by side throughout this treacherous war. Yet, no matter how hard he shook the shoulder of his comrade, he would not move. He was still breathing, shallowly and quickly, but breathing nonetheless. Otto though that perhaps he had been shellshocked, or knocked unconscious by the blast. He checked Kellerman's head and chest for potential injuries, until he came to his neck, and became frozen in that moment.

Kellerman was not breathing, but dying. He was choking on blood pouring into his oesophagus from a piece of shrapnel, at least an inch wide, which had become lodged in his throat. He looked up at Otto for a moment and grasped at the young driver's arm, panicking as he realised the untreatable nature of his wound. His eyes, so often filled with the focus of an alpha hunter, had become flooded with intense fear, a frenzied search for an unattainable solution, as his lungs became increasingly sullied with blood which had begun to pour a crimson waterfall from his gritted teeth. Otto stared back in equal bewilderment, helpless, unable to even articulate that he didn't know what to do. After a few seconds, Kellerman's fighting for air slowed, and a calm came over his face. He took a photograph pinned on the hull next to his loaders seat, and with a trembling hand, placed it in Otto's palm. He then stared him in the eye for a moment, and finally the loader slumped forward, still and unmoving.

The photograph, bloodied and crumpled, sat in Otto's clutches. He unwrinkled the paper to reveal a family photograph. In the centre stood a much younger looking Kellerman, unburdened by the horrors of war, smiling brightly. His wife, a petite young blonde, more beautiful than most, stood next to him with her arms wrapped around his chest. On the chair in front of the couple was a strapping young man, perhaps seventeen years old, with Kellerman's arms upon his shoulders. This was Kellerman's boy, killed so tragically in a bombing raid. His face was filled with promise, excited for what might lie ahead in his life. He was a spitting image of his father. One of the many lives so brutally snuffed out in this new conception of total war; as far as the high commands of each belligerent nation was concerned, every man, woman and child was a legitimate target. This was annihilation.

A bullet pranging into the side of the hull woke Otto from his moment of consideration, and he regained his bearings. After holding of his dear brother in arms one last time, Otto scrambled back through the hatch under the Tiger, and dragged himself through the dirt and gravel to Scholl's position. His comrade had taken to operating the MG42, with no small amount of pain due to his burned hand. The soviet infantry was steadily moving forwards, with each metre paid for in blood, and were now almost within grenade throwing range. Rounds were zipping past the pair's ears at an alarming level of rapidity. Enemy armour was also rolling towards the handful of Panzers, which had mostly run out of ammunition. A grenade thudded softly into the ground of the machine gun pit, which Otto slung out of harm's way with milliseconds to spare. The device cracked with an enormous volume metres away, with the blast shockwaves flying through the two crewmembers. It would be minutes before they were overrun at this rate.

Scholl stopped firing. His gaze was fixed ahead of him, but he appeared uninjured. Otto followed his line of sight, and became stuck fast. A T-34 had finished rotating its turret, and was preparing to shoot the nest. Otto's heart beat in his throat, and his vision narrowed at the edges. This was it. It was strange for Otto to think that this is what the last years had led to; despite the hopes, false promises, early victories, and every expectation of victory, this was it. Fighting tooth and nail within spitting distance of the Reichstag, as the world collapsed around him. The Russians had ensured that Germany reaped what she had so earnestly and brutally sown, and the price was set to fall on every one of the Reich's citizens. A smoke plume erupted from the barrel of the green beast, and Otto's vision went dark.

The ground was soft. Ever so slightly damp, and dusted with ash. The smell reminded Otto of gathering around the fireplace as a child, while his father told him stories about the distant colonies in which he had served.

"In Namibia," he had said, "the trees grow as tall as the sky, and wild animals roam the jungle."

Otto had only been perhaps six or seven years old at the time, and remembered staring up at his father in wonder, amazed at the possibilities of the distant world. The young boy had once wanted to be an explorer, carving his path through the strangest of lands. He felt warm, and the ringing in his ears almost resembled a harmony, a heavenly reprieve. He felt as though he might stay here forever.

Otto opened his eyes, shaken from his reminisces. He was still alive. The situation was as he had left it; machine guns and rifles were still spitting a deadly hail of fire, and their own former machine gun nest had been blown apart by an enemy shell. Otto was laying on his front, facing the Tiger which had grown still, likely knocked out by the same shell which had taken Kellerman. Greim had thrown himself from the turret, and was taking cover behind the hull, issuing pot shots with his rifle. The Soviets continued to advance with war cries and yells, and Scholl was nowhere to be seen. Otto knew he had to help his friend, and so he stood up.

Or, rather, he tried to stand up. But as much as he pushed off from the floor it seemed useless, and he kept crashing back down to the dirt with a thud. It was this point Otto realised a highly unusual sensation; he couldn't feel his legs. He rolled onto his back and pushed his arms to sit and assess the situation. His left leg seemed unharmed, but his right leg had what could best be described as a mangled piece of flesh protruding from where a foot should be. The sight of this gave him quite the shock, not to mention the fact that he could not feel or move either limb. Feeling his back, the young tank driver realised that he was bleeding from there also; a piece of shrapnel had severed his spinal column at the waist. Otto began to hyperventilate, and felt some of the initial adrenaline leave his body in place of weakness.

And then came the pain. Not from his unfeeling lower half, but from the piece of debris lodged in his back, and his head which he had evidently hit in being thrown from the miniature fortification. He began to scream, in a mix of fear and terror; Otto had always imagined that dying would be clear cut, something he was hardly aware of. A stray bullet, and everything would just go dark, painless. But this level of agony, of blind fear and anguish, was not something he had anticipated. Despite seeing hundreds of others die, Otto had convinced himself, as many others have, that his passing wouldn't be so violent. Perhaps that is what had allowed him to willingly place himself in danger so frequently; he had chosen simply not to think about it.

Greim ran to him, and pulled him by the collar to shelter behind the tank. The commander had been shot, high in the shoulder, but appeared hardly to notice. He propped Otto against the Tiger, avoiding placing the shrapnel of his back in any further pain, and began to apply a tourniquet to his shredded leg. His face was emotionless, and he did not meet Otto's gaze.

"Herr Hauptmann," whimpered an ever-weaker Otto. "I… I'm scared."

Greim looked up, and patted his shoulder. "Don't be scared, boy." He smiled, with a fatherly look in his eye. "The show is nearly over now. You'll be out of this blasted war. You have served your country well, even if it betrayed you in turn. It has been an honour to be your commander."

For the first time in his life, Otto saw a tear appear in Greim's eye, and his tone of voice had an element of the farewell in it, an acknowledgement that this would be their last conversation. Once Greim had attached the tourniquet, he handed Otto a water bottle, and went to return to the fight.

But he hesitated, and again knelt beside Otto. He looked him in the eye for a moment, and began fumbling with his tunic. He unpinned his Knight's cross, and affixed it to Otto's uniform.

"If anyone deserves this," he sighed, "it is you."

Then, without further ado, he drew his pistol and rounded the corner of the hull. After a few rounds, he had stopped firing, mown down by an especially close Soviet submachine gun blast. Otto peered through the tracks of the Tiger, and saw his mentor fallen, in a peaceful stillness. The Russians were perhaps seconds away, and Otto prepared to meet his end bravely. There was no use his continuing. As he buttoned his uniform, he caught the feel of something in his pocket. Alexei's letter! He had promised to the Russian that he would do all he could to deliver it! Was this enough to carry on for? Or would it be more fitting for him to pass with his long serving crew?

Time froze, as Otto weighed his options. He made his decision; he would commit the last of his energy to delivering Alexei's letter. If he could find a way to pass it on, there was a chance it would get back to Alexei's partner, and that she would be able to hear her love's last message. He would then, at least, be able to credit himself with one good deed amongst the evil through which they moved. Dipping his fingers into the pooling blood in his sensationless and mutilated leg, he wiped his face until it was sufficiently red to indicate a major injury at a passing glance. He then lay still, as if dead, in his propped position by the tank. Otto clenched his fists as he struggled to steady his breathing against his fear, until finally Russian troops appeared from behind the tank.

Their faces were war-weathered, and twisted in hatred for the regime which they fought. They seemed as though they had not shaved or washed for weeks, but had instead been pushing relentlessly, a struggle etched into the bags which hung dark below their eyes. They continued to lay suppressing fire towards the final German troops, some of whom were being gunned down as they raised their hands to surrender. These men were not inclined to take prisoners. One of the Soviets darted his gaze towards Otto, and fired a machine gun burst at him. Somehow, Otto stayed still, unflinching; he had been unhurt by the attack, except a few bullets which had thumped painlessly into his numbed legs. The squad moved on, and Otto allowed himself a sigh of relief that he had been thought dead, and stifled a sob as the enormity of the situation struck him once more.

They were all dead. His crew, who had guarded his life for years, had all perished. And Otto was sure to join them soon, when he inevitably succumbed to his injuries. Through barely opened eyes, as to maintain the illusion of his being a corpse, he surveyed the scene which lay before him. One of the Russians had thrown grenades into the final King Tiger, holding closed the hatch until muffled explosions had erupted from within. It was now a matter of finishing off any survivors, before they reported the success to their commander. Red Army medics were hurrying about, trying to save as many soldiers as possible now that the danger had passed. Troops were searching the fallen for valuables, and sharing cigarettes and vodka in relief.

A scream began to cut through the air, as an injured German was dragged before one of the Soviet officers. Two burly soldiers threw the poor man at their superior's feet, and one struck him on the head with a rifle butt as he tried to stand up. The officer and soldier exchanged words, until the senior rank waved his hand in dismissal and walked away. As he cleared Otto's line of sight, however, a horrific realisation surfaced; it was Scholl. He was laying between the Soviets and moaning, clearly in terrible pain from the same explosion which had crippled Otto. The Russians were laughing between themselves, gesturing towards Otto's wounded crewmate. Otto knew fully well that he would be unable to save his dear friend; even if he had a weapon within reach, he would be killed before he could act, and Scholl would likely suffer even further for the trouble. He sat still, and tried to avert his attention from what began to unfold.

One of the two men kicked Scholl in the face with great force, causing a spray of blood to shoot from his mouth, while the other soldier continued to punch his torso. The poor gunner had barely the energy left to scream anymore, and instead continued in animalistic groans and grunts, unable to defend himself. What happened next, though, was possibly the most haunting sight Otto had witnessed in the entire war. Bored with their assault, the two men armed themselves; one with an entrenching shovel, and one with a small knife. They laughed some more, encouraging their friends to form an audience for the spectacle. They then yelled into Scholl's ear a broken German warning that this was going to hurt him, for all that he had done to hurt them. His bruised and swollen face did not even react, so exhausted was he. Then, the man armed with the shovel swung it high, and brought it down upon Scholl's skull with tremendous force. A sickening crackling-crunch sound made clear that he had shattered the skull, and Scholl began to make a hollow scowling sound. His eyes were wide open, and he was twitching on the floor; still alive, but his brain had been exposed. The other soldier descended upon him and was stabbing him rapidly, and with great anger, in his ribs. Scholl did not even move in response to this, or hold his arms to defend himself, but let the Soviet carry on, making the same gargling hiss. The Russians which had gathered to witness the show groaned in annoyance that Scholl had died so quickly, and they dispersed along with the two assailants. Scholl was left jerking for a few seconds, before he grew still and silent, finally passing from his suffering.

Otto sobbed at the sight of his friend, so cruelly murdered. He had to restrain himself however, as a Russian strode towards him. The man was clearly drunk, and in search of loot. He climbed aboard the Tiger, and rummaged for a few minutes, before coming back to the MG nest. He was wearing Greim's officers cap, taken from the cabin, and held Kellerman's pipe lit between his teeth. Finally, he crouched beside Otto, and pulled Greim's Knight's Cross from his unform. Otto held his breath for the entire ordeal, sure that he would be detected. But the Soviet simply sauntered away, rich from his plunder, and left Otto to rot. The stress of this proved too much, and Otto began to feel faint once again. His vision steadily grew darker, until he passed into a deep slumber.

Epilogue: Part I
Wittenbergplatz, Berlin

Light began to seep into Kurt's eyes, as the sound of rough bricks and scraping rubble danced through the air; he was being dug out of his shelter. After most of the debris had been cleared, a sooty hand reached through the gap and pulled him free by the collar. Standing before Kurt was a bemused Soviet soldier, who put him down and handed him a canteen of water. His mouth was like cotton, having been trapped in what remained of the house he had chosen to hide in for at least a whole day. A boy of only nine years old, he had been a refugee in Berlin since his mother had died in one of the opening artillery barrages of the city, and he had been forced to hide in a house cleared out by the Volkssturm in order to avoid the fighting. He gulped greedily at the bottle, delighted to quench his thirst. The Russian handed Kurt a morsel of bread, and pointed to an officer who was registering refugees, before he himself stomped off to find the next buried child.

The city was unrecognisable. Hollow half-buildings peppered the skyline, concrete trees against a desert of destruction. Shell holes and debris littered the road on which Kurt now found himself, with one impact crater metres from his former shelter. Exhausted Volkssturm conscripts were being paraded at gunpoint by rifle-wielding Russians, their own weapons seized and uniforms torn. Olive green supply trucks were flooding into the city, in attempts to alleviate the immediate starvation of the populace. Fighter aircraft buzzed past overhead every few minutes, patrolling their latest conquest. Daunted by the transformed settlement before him, Kurt shuffled towards the Tiergarten, hoping to find some destination to reach.

The park was a graveyard. Corpses, and parts of corpses, were scattered across the road, with mangled tanks standing everywhere. There stood leafless stumps where trees had once flourished, stamped dark against the morning's cloud. Gravel crackled under Kurt's battered shoes as he unsteadily trotted on, stepping over the fallen. Soviet soldiers were patrolling the paths, occasionally dragging wounded prisoners away to be treated. He hopped across scorch marks and chunks of earth, unsure exactly where he was going or what he was looking for. What did he hope to discover? His stomach rumbled, and he realised that perhaps that the handful of bread with which he was issued was not quite sufficient to alleviate at least a day or two's hunger. Some refugees had started foraging in the park for nuts or berries, but he was never one for telling what was safe to eat and what wasn't. He would need something he could recognise.

As he closed on the Brandenburg gate, he realised that all around him lay troops with full knapsacks. As a patrol of two soldiers approached, quite clearly drunk and clutching a half empty bottle of vodka each, Kurt tried to ask for some food. He couldn't speak any Russian, and so simply gestured to his mouth and rubbed his tummy. The pair sneered, with one muttering, "Piss off, Hitler spawn," in rather clear German, and continued past him.

He instead began to search abandoned bags, but was

unable to find sustenance, until he saw a group of dead soldiers near an abandoned tank, some metres into the trees off the side of the route.

Kurt approached cautiously, reminded by the constant pattering of distant gunfire that the war was not entirely over just yet. He saw one soldier, a German, who had been struck rather savagely over the head, and stabbed repeatedly; it was a ghastly sight. Kurt winced, pulling the pack free from the back of the corpse as he mumbled an apology for disturbing it. Kneeling on the cold mud, he undid the straps and rummaged through its contents. His first find was a few blocks of chocolate, which, emaciated as he was, he couldn't help but snaffle instantly. There was some water, too, which he set aside for later. He found a strange device, a grenade wrapped in a belt of ammunition, which he put carefully down on the ground, fearful of activating the hellish contraption. Finally, there was a photograph. It depicted a young man, smiling alongside a beautiful woman. They were outside of a cottage, possibly somewhere in the black forest, judging by the foliage. They seemed happy, truly happy, an expression which Kurt had almost forgotten in the last few years.

A rasping cough threw Kurt into panic, as he jumped to his feet and looked for the source. It was followed by a call in a tired yet warm voice.

"Over here, boy," it said. After a couple of fearful seconds, Kurt eyed a figure propped against the metal hulk of the abandoned tank, waving weakly. He walked to him, and saw that he was a German soldier of some kind. His leg was badly injured, and his face was the shade of death. He gestured to the body from which Kurt had retrieved the pack, asking him, "What did you find over there?"

Kurt showed him the small collection, and the man picked up the photograph from his hand.

"Tell you what, I'll trade you," he smiled, handing Kurt a full water canteen in exchange. "What is your name? he asked.

"Kurt Koch, sir," he replied, his voice tremoring nervously.

"Well, Kurt Koch, it is good to meet you," replied the man, quiet with exhaustion. "And I am no sir, I am Otto, Otto Griff. That is my friend Scholl over there, who you took the bag from." Kurt began to apologise profusely for looting his fallen comrade, stumbling over his words as he attempted to explain his deep hunger, but Otto held his hand up to cut him off. "Don't worry, little man," he laughed. "It wasn't doing him any good now was it! Scholl would have wanted you to have it."

The soldier fumbled in his pocket for a moment, until he produced a bloodstained letter. "Now, Kurt, I have a very special task for you," he said, looking into his eyes. "You must take this letter and deliver it to a Russian officer. Can you do that for me?" asked the man. Kurt nodded quickly, which elicited a smile from the wounded soldier. "There is a good lad," he smiled, wincing as he breathed. "Boy, how I would like to tell you my stories, Kurt, but I haven't much time, and you have a special assignment! But allow me to leave you with this: this war started because people didn't think about what they were doing, what would happen. So please Kurt, make sure that you always question the world, never go along blindly. Stay curious, little one," he said, gesturing Kurt to go.

"I will, sir… I mean, um, Otto!" stuttered Kurt, before standing and running down the path from which he had come. Or rather trying to run, as he collided straight into the torso of a Russian soldier. It was the drunk pair from earlier, who had denied him food. Their bumping into one another had caused him to drop his vodka, which smashed on the ground. The soldier's bloodshot eyes widened in fury, and he smacked Kurt across the jaw as he yelled curses at him. He raised his rifle, ready to kill Kurt in his rage, but Otto yelled from the tank to gain the Soviet's attention. Instead of shooting Kurt, the man cycled the bolt of his rifle, and levelled it at the wounded tanker. A sharp crack, and Otto slumped to the side, motionless.

Kurt was far from safe, however, as the soldier then proceeded to ready his weapon and aim it at the boy once more. He winced, and shut his eyes, only to hear two shots rather than the one. Cautiously, Kurt looked up, only to see the pair of soldiers just as confused as he was. The source of the noise was soon revealed; a pistol waving Soviet was running towards them, in a highly decorated officers' uniform. He had fired into the air, and was now barking furious orders at the pair. The two soldiers stood to attention, looking nervously ahead. The officer beat the soldier which had shot Otto, his pistol connecting harshly with his cheek, launching the soldier to the ground. He quickly collected himself, and stood back to attention, wincing in pain and bleeding slightly from his face. The officer then seized the other soldier's bottle of vodka, and gestured for the pair to leave, who swiftly continued their patrol with their tails between their legs.

The officer then crouched to Kurt's height, and took something from his pocket. He was old, war weary, with a bushy grey moustache which curled outwards, and beady brown eyes which sparkled from behind damaged spectacles. He smelt of tobacco and alcohol, but was smiling warmly, and gave Kurt a feeling of safety, not least due to his having saved the boy moments ago. He unwrapped the parcel he had produced from his greatcoat, revealing a portion of salted beef, smelling of hearty spices and sprinkled with herbs. The officer handed it to Kurt with an even greater smile, his rosy red cheeks wide with a chuckle as he saw the starving boy's joyous reaction. He patted Kurt on the back and stood, pointing down the path to a refugee care centre.

The officer went to leave, but Kurt remembered with a sharp intake of breath his mission from Otto. He held out the letter, which the officer took and held his glasses as he read the address. He sighed, looked down to Kurt and nodded in understanding. It was clear that he knew what to do with the letter, and he set off down the Tiergarten path. Kurt, satisfied that he had completed his task, started in the direction of the refugee centre, hoping to find a warm drink.

Epilogue: Part II
Sadovoye Village, USSR

Natalia could hear the humming of engines, and looked out of her damaged window frame to spy a car winding steadily up their country road. The well-polished and sleek vehicle seemed to stand as a striking oxymoron, when compared with their quaint collective farm. Despite being relatively close to Stalingrad, they had seen few vehicles in the area since around 1943, and so a number of the farmers and families lined the road, excited about what might be going on. Natalia turned down the heat on the vegetable broth which she was preparing, and opened the front door to join the spectators. She had not seen her Alexei in about a year, and was hoping for some news as to when the soldiers would be returning home.

  The car pulled up in the middle of the street, and a tall NKVD officer stepped from the vehicle. He held a newspaper aloft, before declaring, "We have taken the fascist lair!"

  The crowd erupted in happiness. There were cheers, tears of joy, and people hugging one another in relief. The farm had lost many people and much livestock to the German invasion, and had been working very hard to keep their Russian soldiers supplied with food at the front. But of greater importance to Natalia was the thought that perhaps Alexei would be home soon.

  The scene of jubilation was contagious, with the warm

spring day and light breeze signalling the dawning of a new era, an era of peace. Natalia's mother, a sweet and short elderly woman, waddled towards her, hunched over as usual, with a toothless grin painted across her happy face. Her husband, Natalia's father, had been killed in the First World War, and she had always feared that the same fate might befall Natalia's lover.

"Is it not wonderful, Natalia!" she exclaimed. "Alexei will come home soon!"

Natalia hugged her mother, tearing up from the joy of it all. The officer was speaking to a few of the farmers, who then pointed in the direction of Natalia. She was curious as to what was being discussed, and the officer then approached her. The smile had retreated from his face, and he now looked at her in stoic sympathy. He handed her two pieces of paper, a telegram and a bloodstained letter. She stood in confusion for a moment; was this a joke of some kind? She looked at her mother, who had grown equally unsettled, her hand clasped over her mouth in shock. The first piece of paper bore the hammer and sickle of a party message, and had one line on it.

"Alexei Simonov. KIA."

Natalia collapsed, screaming. This couldn't be true. The world seemed unreal. The officer and her mother had caught her as she fell, and lowered her gently to the ground, looking on with empathy. Her hearing faded, and she was trapped in that moment. People were yelling in celebration, with some looking uncomfortably at the distraught woman who had been so happy only moments ago. She had waited so long for Alexei to return home, and had always been convinced that he would come back to her arms. It couldn't be true that she had lost him.

2 April 1945.

My darling Natalia,
I hope that this letter finds you well. You will, I am sure, be pleased to hear that I am in good health and spirit. We are well into the borders of Germany now. Each day we get closer to Berlin, and closer to when I shall return to the farm once more.

How is everyone back home? Is your mother still able to do her jobs around the house, or is her health failing with the cold? My comrades are certainly glad of the thaw, not least because our winter coats are proving heavy; the sooner we can discard them, the better. Each day we press kilometres forward. The German still has some fight left in him, however, and we sometimes encounter heavy casualties when we take strategic positions. Breslau is proving a particularly difficult conquest.

Their regime must be collapsing now. I have encountered whole regiments of conscripted boys, no older than sixteen. Our political commissar claims that it's a sign of the fascist corruption, that their nation is being brought down with them. I'm not so sure of politics, I just want to make it back safely to you.

When this war is over, we will come here. To Germany. It will be rebuilt, a world without fascism. I wonder if there will be any collective farms we could move to, perhaps near the Oder. It would do us good to get somewhere where the winters are less harsh, not least on account of your mother's health. The things I have seen, Natalia. Beauty, vast swathes of land ready for the taking. And hell, the furious fire of war, consuming everything as we get closer to the fascist lair.

I will be with you soon. Send your hopes with me as I fight on, for the Motherland. I will bring you back a brick from the Reichstag itself!

Yours,

Alexei.

The officer produced a handkerchief from his pocket and handed it to her. He seemed ill at ease dealing with emotions, but knelt beside her nonetheless, trying to console her. She fought to regain her breath between sobs. This war had taken everything from her. Taking the letter, she tried not to touch any of the dried blood which was encrusted across the paper. It was from Alexei, dated for early April. She opened back the flap of paper, and tried carefully to read it through watery eyes.